"You don't owe me anything, Red. Let's get that straight."

Embarrassment crackled through her. Tessa knew she didn't owe him. But she wanted something from him that she couldn't articulate. Mostly she wanted more of the confidence she'd felt when she was losing herself in his arms.

For those minutes, she wasn't pretending to be somebody new or reaching for a version of herself she wasn't sure she could even live up to. It had all been real and authentic, and she'd liked herself at that moment. She liked herself with him.

"I know that. So I guess this is the point where I say you can hit the road. And don't let the door—"

"I got the message." Carson stood. "I had fun tonight."

"It doesn't mean anything," she felt compelled to say. Another lie.

Dear Reader,

Thank you for choosing this book—whether you're returning to Starlight or this is your first visit to this sweet fictional town, I appreciate you being here. I'm often in awe of people who have overcome major challenges to create the life they want for themselves so I loved bringing Tessa and Carson's story to the pages.

Tessa Reynolds spent much of her life battling chronic illness. It shaped the woman she's become, but she's determined to choose a new path as she settles into life in Starlight, Washington. The friends she's made in this small mountain town help give her the courage to step out of the long shadow cast by her health issues, but it's an unexpected connection with her single dad neighbor and his shy daughter that truly changes everything.

Carson Campbell wouldn't tell you he's struggling as a full-time dad, but Carson learned long ago not to show any sort of weakness. And he certainly doesn't want to admit to his reckless, wild new neighbor that he needs help. But his daughter, Lauren, is drawn to Tessa, and Carson finds himself falling for the redhead. Tessa isn't who she seems and her gentle way with his girl melts the ice around his heart. Neither Carson or Tessa is looking for love, but it just might be what they need to find the happiness they both crave.

I love to hear from readers, so please reach out at michellemajorbooks@gmail.com.

Happy reading!

Michelle

Starlight and the Single Dad

MICHELLE MAJOR

HARLEQUIN
SPECIAL
EDITION

HARLEQUIN®
SPECIAL EDITION™

Recycling programs for this product may not exist in your area.

ISBN-13: 978-1-335-40835-8

Starlight and the Single Dad

Copyright © 2022 by Michelle Major

All rights reserved. No part of this book may be used or reproduced in any manner whatsoever without written permission except in the case of brief quotations embodied in critical articles and reviews.

This is a work of fiction. Names, characters, places and incidents are either the product of the author's imagination or are used fictitiously. Any resemblance to actual persons, living or dead, businesses, companies, events or locales is entirely coincidental.

This edition published by arrangement with Harlequin Books S.A.

For questions and comments about the quality of this book, please contact us at CustomerService@Harlequin.com.

Harlequin Enterprises ULC
22 Adelaide St. West, 41st Floor
Toronto, Ontario M5H 4E3, Canada
www.Harlequin.com

Printed in U.S.A.

Michelle Major grew up in Ohio but dreamed of living in the mountains. Soon after graduating with a degree in journalism, she pointed her car west and settled in Colorado. Her life and house are filled with one great husband, two beautiful kids, a few furry pets and several well-behaved reptiles. She's grateful to have found her passion writing stories with happy endings. Michelle loves to hear from her readers at michellemajor.com.

Books by Michelle Major

Harlequin Special Edition

Welcome to Starlight

The Best Intentions
The Last Man She Expected
His Secret Starlight Baby
Starlight and the Single Dad

Crimson, Colorado

Anything for His Baby
A Baby and a Betrothal
Always the Best Man
Christmas on Crimson Mountain
Romancing the Wallflower
Sleigh Bells in Crimson
Coming Home to Crimson

Visit the Author Profile page
at Harlequin.com for more titles.

To anyone dealing with chronic illness or pain—
I see you and I admire your strength every day.

Chapter One

Tessa Reynolds drew in a deep breath of the steaming air surrounding her then tried to bite back a coughing fit. She concentrated on pulling oxygen in and out of her lungs and reminded herself that this was normal. Nothing more than a little cough. Healthy people did it all the time. It didn't mean anything.

Still, her heart hammered in her chest because Tessa wasn't healthy. Or rather she was now, but even three years of being normal weren't enough to counter two decades of chronic kidney disease.

She dipped her hand into the bubbling surface of the natural hot spring in which she sat. Although it was mid-April in the Cascade Mountains of western Washington, the day had been unseasonably cool. That's part of the reason Tessa had made the mile and a half hike from her cabin to the hot springs she remembered from her childhood.

She hadn't been able to walk the whole way when she was younger, and the memory of her aunt and her sister leaving her behind grated like an itch she couldn't quite scratch.

It was nearly dusk, the temperature dropping fast, and she'd have to leave in a couple of minutes if she was going to make it back up the hill before night fell in earnest.

She might have come to the small town of Starlight in order to reinvent herself, to start over as something other than Tessa the sick girl. To become the wild woman she'd always believed herself to be on the inside. Wild was one thing. Stupid was another, and it would be ten kinds of foolish to stay out in the thick forest past dark.

Her breathing slowed and her lungs stopped constricting. She was almost positive she'd inhaled a bug and that was to blame for her coughing jag.

Then she heard the crack of a branch nearby and went stock-still. It was an animal. It had to be an animal. No one would be out in this part of the mountain except…

"You're trespassing."

She resisted the urge to cover her naked breasts at the sound of the deep voice. Shadows played across the water and the hot springs were naturally dark. Her rational brain knew there was no way the man approaching could see any part of her body other than her shoulders, neck and head. She was as covered as if she were wrapped in a thick blanket.

That didn't stop the nerves from skittering through her.

"I'm most certainly not trespassing," she answered, proud that her voice didn't waver. "We're on my property and you, sir, are both trespassing and rude. This is a private pool and I don't appreciate you being here. Please leave."

Carson Campbell looked around as if she must be talking to somebody besides him. She wasn't about to admit that she recognized him, her surly neighbor who she'd managed to avoid eye contact with since he'd moved into the cabin down the road from hers a month earlier.

"You're on my property," he said. "Although the sir is a nice touch. But get out." His steely gaze tracked to the pile of clothes sitting on a nearby boulder then flicked to her again. "Now."

Tessa wouldn't have guessed it was possible for a man like Carson to get any more intimidating than he was on a regular day. He had an athlete's body with broad shoulders and a muscled chest that tapered into lean hips and hard thighs. Not that she made a habit of noticing male thighs. She happened to be driving through town one day when Carson bent over to pick up something his daughter dropped on the sidewalk.

Tessa had nearly rear-ended the car in front of her.

But he wasn't her type, especially with evening quickly descending. She could clearly make out the frown that pulled his full lips into a thin line. It wasn't fair that he had a mouth like that. Lush and ripe and made for sin. That mouth did not belong on him. Not when his gaze was always so guarded and angry.

A mouth like that should smile and laugh and kiss. Tessa dreamed of being kissed by—

What was she doing? Her stupid penchant for day-dreaming, spinning off into a fantasy world at the most inopportune times, was on full display.

Because while she'd been contemplating Carson's mouth, he'd been moving closer. "Stay back," she yelled then splashed water toward him, a completely ineffectual deterrent.

"You should have considered your modesty before you decided to go skinny-dipping in a place where you're not welcome."

Oh, but if Tessa had allowed being unwelcomed to deter her, she'd have even less of a life than she already did.

"I'm not modest," she said, a blatant lie but she

doubted Carson would be able to see her flaming cheeks with the steam rising around her. Or he'd hopefully blame the color on the hot water. "I'm annoyed." That part was true.

"You're annoyed?" Carson let out a rusty laugh. "That's rich, sweetheart."

"For your information…" She moved across the pool, which was built into the rocks on the side of the mountain, a true natural spring. "I was having a peaceful meditative interlude on my aunt's property. Land that I have every right to occupy."

His thick brows drew together. "Who is your aunt?"

"Marsha Reynolds. She lives in Tucson now. I'm staying at her cabin."

"You're my neighbor." He said the words like an accusation. "The one with the obnoxious red car."

"Julian is an adorable Jeep. Jeeps aren't obnoxious. It's impossible."

"She named her car," he muttered. "Why am I not surprised?"

Before she could answer, he pointed a finger in her direction. "You drive too fast and listen to your music too loud. I've seen you and I don't like it. You're dangerous."

"Do you think so?" Tessa asked, unable to hide her shock. "That's amazing."

"Excuse me?"

"I mean, you have no right to judge me." She kept the smile out of her voice, just barely. "My driving is none of your business, just like me being in this pool is not your concern. My aunt has been coming to this hot springs for as long as I can remember."

"The Realtor told me it was on my land."

"He lied."

"The Realtor is a she."

"The pronoun changes but nothing else." Tessa wanted to be mean, but it really wasn't in her nature and her aunt might have made a mistake. "This land has been in my family for generations. Who knows about the property lines? But what I do know is that I'm not trespassing."

"I'm not either," her bossy new neighbor said definitively. Carson Campbell was a certified grump. Had Tessa ever sounded that sure of herself?

"You should leave anyway. I don't appreciate you looming over me like some sort of malevolent threat."

"You think I'm a threat?" Carson asked, his voice silky smooth.

To her equilibrium undoubtedly. But she wasn't about to admit that. "I don't scare easily," she lied. Most of her life had been spent in fear. Fear of being sick or weak or having her body give out on her. And in the moments she'd forgotten to be scared, her family had been more than willing to take up the reins of that particular horse. If Tessa's mother had her way, her younger daughter wouldn't have left the house unless she was encased in a thick roll of bubble wrap.

Tessa hadn't talked to her mom since moving to Starlight, and she missed her. They exchanged texts that more often than not resulted in her mother sending long, lecturing messages about Tessa taking care of herself and being safe.

It was easy enough to ignore the messages, but Tessa didn't want to hear the worry in her mom's voice or deal with the fact that no one in her family believed that at twenty-seven, she was capable of living on her own.

"Maybe I came down here to use the hot springs," he said. "How do you feel about company?"

There was a teasing lilt to his voice, but even Tessa had her limits. "No thanks." The two words came out as more of a squeak than a sentence.

One corner of Carson's delicious mouth lifted, as if all of her posturing had been for naught. Like he knew she was a born and bred coward no matter how she acted.

Fear might have been Tessa's most stalwart companion over the years, but that didn't make her hate it any less.

"I'm done here anyway. It's getting dark. I need to get home. Big plans for the night and all that."

"I'm sure," Carson agreed. He folded his arms over his chest but didn't move.

"What are you doing?" she demanded.

One bulky shoulder rose and fell. "The rocks are slippery. I figured I'd wait and make sure you got out okay." He lifted her sweatshirt off the boulder. "I'm sure anyone who goes skinny-dipping in the middle of the woods isn't a big proponent of modesty."

Heat burned through Tessa. She could tell by the gleam in his eye that he was calling her out. Calling her bluff.

It was as if the past few months and all the new things she'd done and the courage she'd discovered vanished in an instant. This infuriating man saw her for who she was and, as always, she came up lacking.

"But if you need privacy…"

"No." The word came out on a husky breath. If she wasn't mistaken, a shiver passed through Carson. She'd well and truly shocked him, and the knowledge of it fanned the spark of her bravery into a white-hot flame.

Before she could think better of it, she stood, hoping the shadows would prevent Carson from truly noticing the details of her body as she made this stand…literally. Her knees were shaking, but she didn't let that stop her. She gasped as the cool night air hit her naked body. The difference in temperature between in the water and out was jarring. Goose bumps rose along her arms and legs, and she felt her nipples pucker in the cold.

Or was that a reaction to the way Carson's stormy gaze went molten?

He tossed the sweatshirt in her direction and spun on his heel. "Woman, you have no sense. You can't just stand up naked in front of a stranger."

She scrambled out of the pool and tossed her sweatshirt over her head then stepped into her sweatpants, not bothering with underpants or the bra. "We're neighbors," she reminded him. "You're not exactly a stranger."

"Even so," he ground out.

"I'm glad we had this little talk," she said, trying to sound bolder than she felt. "At first glance, I wouldn't peg you for a stick-in-the-mud. Good to know you are. I'm not interested in getting to know people like you."

"The feeling is mutual." She could see his hands clenched at his sides even in the dim light and decided she needed to get out of there before he realized how big of a liar she truly was.

"Have a good night, neighbor." She toed on her gym shoes and headed up the trail.

Tessa might want adventure in this new chapter of her life, but she realized her inherent self-preservation instinct remained intact. Nothing in the world could have forced her to turn around and look at Carson Campbell again.

* * *

Carson slammed the door of his cabin behind him then cringed when his daughter, Lauren, startled and knocked over the glass of water sitting in front of her on the kitchen table.

"Sorry, Laur," he said as he rushed forward.

"Oh, my God, Dad. My math homework is ruined."

"We can fix it," he promised, although he wasn't certain he could handle even this one small catastrophe, let alone the mountain of challenges resting on his shoulders at the moment.

If a few months of full-time parenting had taught him one thing, it was to keep moving forward. Keep moving—period. He grabbed a roll of paper towels and began blotting at the sopping wet math worksheet. "At least this is a better excuse than the dog ate my homework," he said as Lauren moved her other papers and textbooks out of the way.

"I didn't need an excuse," she told him in the annoyed tone he'd become so used to hearing. "I did the homework."

"And it will dry." He lifted the slip of paper and tried not to wince as a trickle of water dripped from the edge.

He blamed this mess, along with his jumbled emotions, on his irritating—if gorgeous—neighbor. He didn't even know her name, he realized as he carried the math homework into the laundry room and used a wooden clothespin to hang it on the drying line.

He was well aware of the stranger. Her flaming hair, which matched her cherry red car, was hard to miss.

It had irritated him—*she* had irritated him—on sight. There was a time in his life when Carson had appreciated a bad girl. He'd liked the adrenaline rush of drama and found himself caught up with women who appreciated the same in him.

His need for adrenaline to make him feel alive was what had first led him to the navy and flight school. But he'd grown up during his time in the military. Grown up and past his penchant for trouble.

He didn't make stupid decisions anymore. Or rather he didn't make them on purpose.

He'd made the dumbest decision of his life with the blind faith that his ex-wife was taking care of the daughter they shared.

They'd been too young to get married. That much was clear now, but many of his friends in the squadron had been settling down in their early twenties. Carson had figured putting a ring on Delilah's finger was the logical thing to do after she'd ended up pregnant a few months into their tumultuous relationship.

And as much as she loved Lauren, Delilah had chafed under the constraints of being a navy wife. She simply wasn't cut out for it and blamed Carson for selling her a false bill of goods. He still didn't understand how it was his fault that she'd assumed real life was like something out of *Top Gun*. All smart white uniforms and being serenaded in bars, and not as much deployment and service and the rigors of military life.

Maybe he should have done a better job of preparing her, but that would have been difficult since he'd had no idea what he was getting into until he was there. But he'd thrived on the structure and the duty.

So much so that when Delilah left him and filed for full custody of their nine-month-old daughter, he hadn't even considered fighting her. How was he supposed to take care of a baby and his career at the same time?

For the next decade, he'd done his best to be a decent, if somewhat absentee, father. He'd never missed a childcare payment or a birthday. He sent Lauren gifts from his different ports of call. During the few weeks of downtime he got, he made time for her.

He'd become a cliché. The long-distance dad who tried to make up for not being a real part of his daughter's life with gifts and Disney vacations. In the meantime, he'd ignored the warning signs about his ex-wife. Marriage number two and marriage number three. The fact that her house address changed even more often than the ring on her finger.

Then just before Christmas, he'd received a panicked call from his daughter. It was a miracle he'd had service that night out in the middle of the Pacific Ocean. Lauren had tearfully told him that Delilah was getting married for a fourth time and embarking on a European tour with her soon-to-be rocker husband right after the holidays.

She was sending their daughter to live with an aunt she'd never met before. Delilah had hated her rural Kentucky roots, and Carson at first hadn't believed she would seriously consider leaving their child behind. Carson also hadn't known how he was going to help. But when he tried to explain as much to Lauren, she let out a world-weary sigh and muttered something about her mom being right that he wouldn't want her either.

Talk about being gutted.

He'd upended his life, resigned his commission and picked her up in a hotel in Atlanta on Christmas Eve.

An old navy buddy had gotten him a job as a pilot in Washington state and here they were. Here he was failing every single day just like his ex-wife had told him he would because he could do discipline and training but being a caring human seemed to be beyond his scope of expertise.

Just like his parents had always told him.

But Carson wasn't the troublemaker he'd been as a teenager. He might not know what the hell he was doing as a father, but he was damn sure going to figure it out.

One thing he knew for certain was that it wouldn't involve any fierce and fiery women being part of his sweet, shy daughter's life.

He'd seen the way Lauren's gaze followed the red Jeep when she was out in the front yard as it drove past their house. He imagined the driver with her thumping music and flowing red hair seemed exciting, especially since Lauren had grown up with a mom who thrived on any sort of feverish thrill.

Carson couldn't deny the way his heartbeat picked up speed as well. His gorgeous neighbor threw him off-balance and he was already floundering for purchase in almost every area of his life.

He couldn't take any more disturbances to the calm, quiet, stable home he was trying to build.

His decision to bait her tonight in that hot springs had been another colossal mistake because now he couldn't get the image of her rising out of the steaming water like some sort of modern-day siren.

"Stick with multiplication and division," he said aloud, forcing himself to concentrate on his daughter's homework. Anything to distract himself from his neighbor.

"Dad, is it going to be okay?" Lauren asked quietly from the door to the laundry room.

Her soft tone was filled with doubt, and he hated

that she had no reason to believe in him. He was determined to be the kind of father she could trust no matter what he had to sacrifice to accomplish it.

"It sure is, baby girl. It sure is."

Chapter Two

Two days later, Tessa slammed shut the door to her Jeep, which she'd parked on an empty side street of downtown Starlight. She stretched her arms above her head and opened her mouth wide but no sound came out other than a whisper of breath. Pent-up frustration made her want to scream, but she'd spent so many years tamping down her emotions. They felt trapped inside her.

It was a perfect spring day with blossoms sprouting on trees and the smell of renewal in the air. Too bad the beautiful day was at odds with her black mood. She'd felt this way since her run-in with Carson in the forest.

The man was infuriating, and she remained equal parts embarrassed that she'd put herself on display for him and annoyed that he'd pushed her to the point of feeling that sort of shame. When she'd first come to Starlight, Tessa had had a bucket list of things she wanted to do and another more important list of traits she wanted to leave behind.

Embarrassment at herself and her body was definitely high on the leave-in-the-past list. She'd taken steps in the direction of changing her life and her personality to be the kind of woman she wanted to be. Now she had to admit those changes had been easy because she hadn't been presented with any real challenges. Her crusty neighbor was definitely a challenge.

Not one she could deal with at the moment as she was late to meet her friends for their scheduled lunch date.

Friends. The thought of the women who had become integral in her life made her feel slightly better.

They knew her as the woman she wanted to be, or at least she hoped they did. A notion flitted across her sleep-deprived mind that maybe she wasn't fooling them just like she hadn't fooled Carson.

She put aside the worry. Fake it till you make it and all that. She entered Trophy Room, Starlight's most popular bar and the establishment in town that happened to serve the best food around. Several of the regulars and Tanya, the bartender, waved and called out greetings.

"They're in the back," Tanya told her. "But be warned, Madison's fish order didn't come in and she's on a bit of a rampage."

"So it's basically a regular Friday?" Tessa winked.

"Just about," Tanya agreed with a laugh. "Can I get you anything? Your usual with an extra cherry?"

"Yes, please." Much of the discontent of the past two days faded as she approached the table where Ella Samuelson and Cory Hall already sat.

"What do you think about hyacinths?" Cory asked as Tessa slid into the seat across from her.

"They're beautiful."

"My grandmother grew them back in Michigan." Cory's gaze was soft. "I'm thinking of carrying them in my bouquet."

"Flowers are stupid," Ella said. "They die."

Cory stared at their friend while Tessa reached out and patted Ella's arm. "Our resident romantic," she murmured. "Tomorrow is your ex-boyfriend's wedding, right?"

Ella rolled her eyes. "We were never even boyfriend and girlfriend. We're work colleagues." She did exaggerated air quotes. "And now I'm his best man."

"Woman," Cory clarified.

"What's it matter? He only thinks of me as one of the guys."

"Then he's not worth your time," Tessa reminded her. "Because you are flipping amazing."

Ella stared at her for a moment then nodded. "Yeah. I am. We all are." She shifted her gaze to Cory. "I'm happy for you and you will be a beautiful bride carrying your beautiful flowers. Ignore me."

"Personally, I'd like to ignore all of you except you keep showing up here."

Tessa and Cory shared a smile as Madison Mauer, the fourth member of their little posse of friends and the reason this small sports bar was making a name for itself, approached the table. Madison had been an acclaimed chef in Seattle but she'd come to Starlight when her high-pressure job in a fancy downtown restaurant had become too much for her.

The big city's loss was Starlight's gain as far as Tessa—and most other residents of the town—were concerned. Madison was gifted, although her surly attitude with her employees and patrons alike left something to be desired.

Cory, whose fiancé, Jordan Schaeffer, owned Trophy Room, did her best to soften Madison's rough edges. For her part, Tessa envied those edges. She felt like she had a lot to learn from Madison's tough, take-no-guff personality.

She also knew that her friend's hard shell shielded

a heart as big as the night sky, one that Madison protected at all costs.

"Here's your drink," a waitress said as she placed a glass in front of Tessa. "Tanya added an extra cherry. Can you do that trick where you tie a knot in the cherry stem with your tongue? My older sister taught me when I was in high school."

"I've never mastered it," Tessa said as she plucked a cherry from her pink drink and popped it into her mouth.

"No adult should order a Shirley Temple with a straight face," Madison said with a sniff. She gave the waitress a look that clearly told her to go away, and the young woman hurried back to the bar with a small yelp.

"I thought you were over scaring the staff," Cory said with an exasperated sigh.

"Something got messed up with my weekly order from Seattle, and half of it didn't make it here today. I'm going to be scrambling to come up with the ingredients I need to get the kitchen through the weekend. Basically, it's been a lousy day." Madison tugged on the end of her long blond ponytail. "I need to let off a little steam."

"Not that way," Cory insisted.

"Fine." The chef turned and shouted across the bar, "I can do the cherry trick in case you were wondering. We can compare knots later."

The waitress's eyes widened and she took an involuntary step back.

"Who let you out of the kitchen?" Tanya called. "Leave the front of the house to me, Mauer."

Madison opened her mouth to offer what Tessa assumed would be a scathing reply but closed it again when Cory shook her head.

"You can do the cherry thing, too?" Tessa asked then flicked her gaze toward Ella. "What about you?"

"Yep."

She looked at Cory.

"Don't worry. I'm with you. Actually I've never even tried, because chances are good that if I put a cherry stem in my mouth I'd end up choking on it."

Tessa figured her luck would be about the same but she didn't say that out loud. She loved Cory, but her sweet-tempered friend was nearly as sheltered as Tessa. Madison and Ella both had more experience and a lot more audacity. That's what Tessa wanted for herself.

"I'm going to learn," she said as she placed the cherry stem on her tongue. "I bet I could find YouTube tutorial videos on it." Her voice was slightly garbled as she tried to manipulate the stem.

"Is this another notch on your good-girl-gone-bad bedpost?" Madison asked, sounding amused. "When are you going to learn that you don't have anything to prove, Pollyanna?"

"Don't call me that," Tessa said then went back to chewing on the cherry stem. So much for her friends believing her to be the wild woman she wanted to become. But she wasn't a Pollyanna. She'd had plenty to deal with in her life and didn't always have the sunniest disposition, although her natural tendency was toward optimism.

Cory and Ella went back to discussing details of the upcoming wedding while Madison looked on with a sneer. Every once in a while she would offer a suggestion, most of them thoughtful and romantic which made Tessa know that they were all hopeless romantics at heart.

"Hey, Mad, can I talk to you about the problem with today's order? I think I have an idea how to fix it."

Tessa gulped in a breath at the sound of the familiar deep voice behind her.

Of course, that meant she also choked on the cherry stem. She felt a firm thwack between her shoulder blades as she choked and sputtered with the offending stem lodged in her throat.

Her friends expressed concern and swayed closer, but it was Carson's touch she couldn't seem to shy away from. After what felt like embarrassing hours of public humiliation, the cherry stem popped out of her mouth onto the table.

"Are you okay?" Cory asked.

"Fine," Tessa said with as much cheer as she could muster, taking a long drink of water. "I'm fine," she repeated when Carson continued to rub her back. The touch was far more comforting than it should have been.

"You know you're not supposed to eat the stem," he pointed out, none too helpfully.

"She was tying it in a knot with her tongue," Madison offered, and Tessa wanted to kill her friend.

"That's a dumb trick," Carson muttered.

"Exactly," Cory agreed. "And clearly dangerous."

"I'm fine." Tessa gritted her teeth.

Madison took a step closer to Carson. "I'm going to have trouble with fish taco Friday when I don't have any fresh fish. I can't believe the supplier in Seattle didn't have it ready to go this morning."

"I know. That's why I'm here." He cleared his throat. "The other pilot is booked this afternoon, but I cleared my schedule and arranged for Lauren to stay at the aftercare program at school. I'm doing another run to Seattle and should be back by four."

"Really?" Tessa was shocked when Madison offered Carson a wide grin then threw her arms around his neck for a quick hug. "You are my hero."

Tessa couldn't help the snort of disbelief that escaped her lips.

"Hero, my foot," she said under her breath.

"Did you say you scraped your foot on the trail?"

he asked, his tone irritatingly innocent. "You should be more careful out in the woods."

Madison looked between the two of them, her delicate brows raising. "You two know each other?"

Tessa would have denied it. But Carson took a step around the table and nodded. "We're neighbors. I found her skinny-dipping in the hot springs the other night."

"Oh, Tessa." Ella clapped her hands together. "That was on your bucket list, right?"

"I'm not talking about that." Tessa managed to keep her voice neutral. "With any of you." She settled her glare on Carson, who couldn't seem to hide his smirk. "Especially not you."

He shrugged. "I told you it was a bad idea."

"Because you are a pushy, judgmental jerk."

Both Ella and Cory looked shocked and Madison laughed. "No, offense, Tessa, but your man radar is way off. Carson here is one of the good guys."

"Not one of my good guys," Tessa answered, wondering why she was being so contrary. The guy hadn't done anything to her and she should like that he thought she was somebody different than she knew herself to be. That's what she wanted. Total reinvention in this town. But she couldn't let him get under her skin any more than he already had. That was way too much already.

"Ladies, I'll catch you later. Turns out I've lost

my appetite for lunch." She purposely did not make eye contact with Carson. "Who knows? I might take a quick dip in the hot springs tonight before I start my big weekend plans." She wondered if one of her friends would call her out on the lie. As far as they knew, she spent most weekend nights watching her favorite movies or reading. And that had been true until recently, but she still wasn't ready to share those details.

Somehow she knew they wouldn't approve of her new side hustle.

"That's right." Madison looked like she was trying to contain a smile. "Big wild weekend plans."

Out of the corner of her eye, Tessa saw Carson's mouth pull down at the sides. For all he knew, Madison was telling the truth, and Tessa did have big weekend plans. She certainly wasn't going to be the one to disabuse him of that notion.

She took a long last drink of her Shirley Temple then started for the door.

"What about our Chop It Like It's Hot lunch?" Ella called.

"Rain check," Tessa said with a wave of her hand. She hated that she was allowing Carson Campbell to chase her from her lunch date with her friends. But there was no doubt that despite all of her bluster and a bone-deep commitment to being someone different, at her core Tessa remained a coward.

* * *

Later that evening, Carson parked in front of the popular biker bar in a neighboring town about forty minutes from Starlight. Lauren had been invited to a sleepover at a classmate's house and he'd agreed to let her go. He knew that friends and sleepovers were what normal kids did and it made his heart happy that his daughter was finding her way in this town. At least at school and with friends.

Their relationship remained taut with tension. One wrong move or comment or door slammed that caused homework to be ruined could send her into a tailspin. At the start of the year, he'd talked to a psychologist he'd known from his time in the military. Carson wasn't lying when he said he'd do anything to make things right with his daughter.

The woman, who he'd also happened to date casually when they'd been stationed on the same aircraft carrier, had explained the stages of grief and what happened when a child felt rejected by one of her parents.

For all of Carson's strength and training, it seemed as though there was nothing he could do to remedy the way he and Delilah had screwed up with their daughter. Nothing but move forward, and he was an expert at pushing aside pain in order to propel himself into the future. He nodded at a heavily tattooed

older man who weaved his way through the somewhat seedy bar's parking lot.

He still wasn't sure why he'd chosen this particular establishment for his rare evening out.

Trophy Room would have been a better choice
with locals and visitors to Starlight frequenting the
sports bar. He'd even become friends of a sort with
the bar's owner, Jordan. He also had a connection
with Madison, the bar's cranky but talented chef.

Carson flew in fresh seafood for her every week
as well as supplies for a few other local businesses,
and her gruff personality and exacting standards
amused him.

He thought they were like birds of a feather—people who didn't need other people. True loners. But
she'd shocked him earlier today by giving him one
hell of a tongue-lashing after his flame-haired neighbor beat a hasty retreat from the bar. It wasn't as if
Tessa—because he'd gathered that was her name—
Tessa's little snit of temper had anything to do with
him. He guessed she was going to do whatever par-
tiers did before they tied one on for the weekend.

Madison and the other two women she'd left behind hadn't exactly seen it that way and it irritated
him that he was the one left feeling bad for doing
nothing but calling things as he saw them.

That was why he'd chosen this out-of-the-way bar.
He wanted to have a drink and forget about Tessa

as well as the picture-perfect life he was trying to create for his daughter when he had no idea how to truly make things right.

He let himself into the bar where the sound of loud music and the scent of stale beer and cold sweat assailed his senses.

Yep, this was what he needed to forget about life for at least a couple of hours. He made his way through the crowd of people, a mix of shaggy-haired twentysomethings and legitimate bikers, all of them clearly with the same focus of starting the weekend with a party.

Some people might find this crowd intimidating but not Carson.

He'd spent a good portion of his childhood in bars similar to this one, tagging along with his dad after work in whatever city they were stationed in during Jacob Campbell's long military career.

He wasn't complaining. The adults had been kind to him. They'd given him money for the jukebox and bowls of popcorn and let him sneak french fries off their plates. Unfortunately, there had been some scary moments for a kid. Times when things got out of hand, but he'd been smart enough to hide under tables or make himself scarce when the energy grew restless.

His dad had always been in the middle of things, unable to ever back down from a fight. Carson had been on that same track until the college counselor in his high school had suggested he'd be a good candidate for the navy. He hadn't expected to follow in his father's footsteps, but he owed that counselor, Mrs. Simpson.

He owed a lot of people.

Despite making peace with his unorthodox childhood, he didn't want the same thing for Lauren. He wanted her to have a normal, happy life. Birthday parties with sprinkled cupcakes, and pony rides, and whatever else it was that girls from mainstream homes enjoyed.

He was giving that to her, but occasionally he craved the comfort of the familiar. A bar like this was as familiar to him as his own skin.

"You new around here?" the man on the stool next to him asked while he wiped a leathered hand across his mustache to get rid of the traces of beer foam.

"I live over in Starlight," Carson answered, unable to hide the pride in his voice. He'd never dreamed he'd be able to claim that he belonged anywhere let alone an idyllic town like Starlight.

"It's pretty there," the man said. "Quiet, though."

"I like quiet."

"Yet here you are."

"Yeah. Here I am."

"You know Tessa?"

A ripple of unease went through Carson. There

was no possible way this man could be talking about his neighbor. None whatsoever.

He drained his beer as he shook his head. "Doubt it."

"Funny." The man shrugged. "I thought she came over from Starlight, too. Not that she talks much about herself. Believe me, I've tried. Everybody has tried. I've watched more men make a fool of themselves over Tessa since she started working here than I've seen in all of my days."

The unease blossomed to full-fledged panic. He could imagine only one woman who might inspire that sort of idiocy in an entire bar of men.

Then a flash of red hair caught his eye, and Carson knew this night was about to go downhill fast.

"Nice talking to you," he said to the man next to him as he pushed back from the bar. "Gotta go."

He'd only taken a few steps when Tessa crossed his path. She wore a tight jean skirt and a top so short that a strip of fair skin was visible between the hem and the top of the denim. Her hair had been curled and fell in loose waves around her shoulders, and her big blue eyes were lined with dark kohl. She looked different and familiar and it felt like all of Carson's secret fantasies had come to life in this woman.

"You," she breathed.

"You don't belong here," he blurted before he thought better of it.

"I work here."

"Even so."

"I'm not any of your business, Carson."

"I know, which is why I'm leaving." He stared at her for another long moment, willing her to walk away first. It didn't surprise him that she didn't budge.

And he wanted her more because of it. So he turned and walked away as fast as his legs would carry him.

Chapter Three

Tessa drove home in the wee hours of the night—actually the early hours of the morning since the bar where she waitressed did last call at 2 a.m.

As she headed up the winding mountain road that led to her cabin, she couldn't help but think about Carson and the way he'd looked at her tonight. She might not have a lot of experience with men, thanks to spending most of her teenage years and early twenties in and out of the hospital, but she understood desire.

There was no doubt in her mind that Carson's enigmatic gaze had held desire for her. She'd be a liar if she said she didn't get a little rush that someone like him could want somebody like her. Even if it was the wild part of her that attracted him, she must be doing something right.

In truth, the job at the dive bar was good for her. It gave her confidence or at least it was bolstering her confidence. She wasn't sure what had made her apply that afternoon a month ago when she'd driven by on her way out of Starlight. She had even less of a clue what had possessed the manager to give her a chance.

Although he'd made it very clear that the baggy T-shirt and shorts she'd worn into the bar that day weren't going to cut it. It had given her quite a thrill to order a few denim miniskirts and crop tops online. Clothes she would never have the guts to wear in her real life.

She still wondered what had possessed Carson to show up there. He clearly hadn't known he would run into her and he didn't seem like the type to frequent a biker bar—even one that she suspected was on the tame side given the location.

She made the turn onto the dead-end street that led to her cabin. A light at the side of the road caught her eye. As she drew closer, she realized it was Carson standing at the end of his driveway waving her down. She could have blown right by. Maybe she should have.

Instead she slowed to a stop and rolled down her

window as he came around the front of the car. Her headlights accentuated the muscles of his legs, which were covered in the same faded denim he'd been wearing earlier. He frowned at her, and she resisted the urge to fidget.

"Is there a problem or were you just looking to give me more grief? Because it's been a long night and I need a shower and a warm bed." The air between them grew charged at her words.

Oh, Lord. Could he possibly think she was inviting him into the shower with her? This was the problem with being inexperienced. She didn't really know how to talk to men. She was learning, but Carson seemed to be a different story. He put her on edge in a way she couldn't explain. She tried to tell herself she didn't like it, but that was a flat-out lie.

"I'm sorry if I came on too strong."

"Wait just a minute." She turned off her car and stepped out, offering him a wide grin as she leaned closer. "I couldn't hear you clearly. Would you repeat those words?"

"I came on too strong."

"No, the other words. The ones where you apologized. Not the best apology I've ever heard, by the way," she said, tapping one toe against the dirt road.

He drew in a deep breath. "I'm sorry for how I acted. And for how I was at the hot springs the other night. I don't know what it is about you that pushes my buttons, but that's my problem. It's not fair to take it out on you."

Tessa's heart did a quick stutter inside her chest. She pushed his buttons. Wasn't that interesting? She'd never been somebody who pushed anyone's buttons and found the idea of it appealed to her. Especially with this man. "The Thirsty Chicken is a nice place, and I get to make the decision whether to work there."

"I'll debate the nice part but not your right to work there. We're neighbors and it's none of my business how you spend your time or who with."

"Exactly," she agreed.

She didn't mention that certain parts of her were big fans of it being his business.

"My daughter..." He glanced back at the house. "She's young and impressionable. Her mom wasn't a great role model, and it took me a while to realize how bad things had gotten."

Tessa frowned. She could deal with verbal sparring and Carson's holier-than-thou attitude, but she didn't like the note of vulnerability in his voice. She didn't want any reason to feel something other than animosity and physical attraction for him.

"I don't even know your daughter." It wasn't exactly true. She'd seen the cute blonde girl in the front yard several times as she'd driven by. The kid always ran to the edge of her yard and waved. Tessa thought she seemed sweet.

"I'd like to keep it that way," Carson told her, his voice taking on a hard edge. "I don't want her to have anything to do with you."

Strangely that stung. Tessa liked kids. She'd volunteered for a local kidney foundation in high school. Working with boys and girls younger than her who were dealing with similar health issues to the ones she'd been going through.

"What makes you think I want to have anything to do with your daughter?"

She took a step closer to him. Anger at the insinuation that she was bad news for a child bubbled up inside her. Maybe she was being a hypocrite.

She wouldn't have let her childhood self near the woman she was trying to be. But taking risks and reinventing herself didn't mean she wasn't a good person.

That was another thing she'd learned from a month working at the biker bar, not to judge a book by its cover. She'd certainly been judged enough in her life in the opposite way.

"Maybe you don't. She's had a lot to deal with over the years," Carson said, sounding resigned. Tessa liked him fighting more than she liked him resigned. "I don't want her hurt and disappointed. People who run on adrenaline tend to fizzle out fast."

Now was not the time for her to explain that she was more boring than brash. She'd never thought about the possibility that life could give her what she wanted and it wouldn't exactly turn out the way she'd expected.

"If you try to box her in, she's going to rebel." Tessa knew that better than most.

"You don't understand."

Oh, but she did. This wasn't her fight, though. She had to remind herself that she had enough to deal with in her own life. Carson Campbell and his daughter were none of her business.

"I'll stay away from her," she told him. "No problem. Heck, I won't even wave to her if it makes you happy."

"Heck," he repeated, his full mouth curving into a smile. "You're funny."

"A real laugh riot," she agreed. "Scratch that. I will wave to her if she waves to me because that's polite."

He threw back his head and chuckled. "I'm sure manners are important to you."

"As a matter of fact, yes. Wild women can still display proper manners. There's no law against that."

He moved closer. To her surprise, he reached out a finger to tuck a strand of hair behind her ear. The touch was featherlight and his finger warm and calloused. Awareness shot through her like a bullet. And he wanted to talk about danger? What a laugh.

"Just stay away from me and my daughter," he said. "Please."

Tessa nodded, unable to form an actual sentence when he was so close. She could smell the woodsy scent of him. In the glow from her headlights, she could see flecks of gold she hadn't noticed previously in his gray eyes. It would be better for both of them if she steered clear.

Somehow she couldn't force herself to turn for her car. It was as if there were an invisible thread holding her close to Carson. She could take all the risks she wanted, but there was no doubt that being near this man was the most dangerous thing she'd ever done.

Because he was smarter, he broke their connection. "Good night, Tessa," he said quietly.

"Yeah," she agreed and hurried to the vehicle. She turned it on and hit the accelerator too hard, sending a flurry of dust into the air. She didn't watch to see Carson's reaction.

Carson sped down the road that led to his house the following week muttering curses that would have made his third-grade teacher blush. Desperate times called for desperate language.

He'd made a routine flight to Portland for medical supplies for the local hospital. The weather forecast early that morning had been perfect so he hadn't given much thought to his return. But the weather changed quickly in this part of the country. By the time he loaded up the plane, he was looking at nearly zero visibility and a thunderstorm moving in.

Part of him had wanted to take the chance because of what a delay would mean for his daughter, but he knew better than to take risks anymore. There was simply too much at stake. He'd called Lauren's school only to be informed that the aftercare program was filled for that day, something he hadn't even realized could happen.

Then he'd dialed the mom of the teenage babysitter he'd hired a few times. The girl had been scheduled for a tennis match that afternoon, another unexpected wrinkle. Panic had started to set in.

Was this the plight of single parents everywhere? The pressure of being the only one on the hook for their child. Feeling desperate, he'd called Madison at Trophy Room. He couldn't imagine the cantankerous chef babysitting, but what choice did he have?

He'd kept to himself in town and didn't have many other friends outside of her and Jordan. Jordan had been next on his list because Carson had figured his fiancée might be willing to step up and help. Madison hadn't exactly laughed, but she'd told him there was no way she could leave work. It was a playoff night, and the bar was already wall-to-wall people according to her.

Then she told him to hold on for a minute. When she came back on the line, she'd shocked the hell out of him by reporting that Tessa Reynolds could pick up Lauren from school and keep her until Carson returned.

Didn't the universe just have the sickest sense of humor? The woman he'd actually warned to stay away from his daughter would be the one he had to rely on to rescue him.

He couldn't figure out why Tessa would have said yes. It wasn't as if she liked him any more than he liked her, and she told him she had no interest in making friends with his kid. But she'd agreed, so Carson had alerted the school to add her to the pickup list for Lauren.

He'd hoped he'd only be an hour late, but it had taken most of the afternoon for the heavy Pacific Northwest fog to burn off. Although he'd left as soon as he was able, it was nearly six by the time he parked in Tessa's driveway.

He hadn't seen her house up close before this. Because she was at the end of the road, he had no reason to venture down this far until now. The cabin was smaller than his with a porch that ran along the front complete with two painted rocking chairs and a sign that welcomed friends. Those homey touches had to be left over from her aunt. He couldn't imagine Tessa—biker-bar waitress and unapologetic skinny-dipper—as the type to concern herself with feathering her nest. Once again, he reminded himself that she'd done him a huge favor today.

No matter what he thought of the woman, he owed her big-time. As he approached the front porch, he realized that part of his problem was the conflicting feelings he felt toward Tessa. He definitely didn't want anybody with a penchant for wild-woman tendencies in his daughter's life. But he couldn't deny his attraction. That was dangerous to the steady and staid life he was trying to create in Starlight.

He knocked on the door, and his breath caught as Tessa answered. She wore a baggy sweatshirt, work-out pants and her hair was pulled up into a high bun on top of her head. She didn't seem to be wearing any makeup, and for a moment her gaze was so open he felt like he might pitch off the edge of the world as he knew it and fall into the depths of her eyes.

He wasn't sure who she was expecting, but as she took him in, her gaze grew guarded. He wanted to growl in protest. But that would be stupid. Carson liked to think he'd left stupid behind.

"You're glaring at me like I kidnapped her," she said, crossing her arms over her chest as she stepped back to let him in. "Do I need to remind you that I did you a favor this afternoon?"

So much for falling.

"Nope. I'm grateful."

He closed the door behind him, taking a moment to try to regain his equilibrium. Then he turned back and glanced over her shoulder. "I don't hear anything. Tell me my kid isn't locked in the closet or under the stairs."

Tessa rolled her eyes. "Nothing so sinister," she assured him. "We're finishing up a project in the kitchen."

She led him down a narrow hallway. "This is a cute cabin," he said as they walked past a cozy sitting room complete with a stone fireplace and an overstuffed couch.

"My aunt takes the credit. There wasn't much I had to do. I'm grateful to her for letting me rent the place. It was a vacation property before I moved in, and she made a lot more money that way."

"But you're family. I bet she wants to take care of you."

Tessa let out a harsh laugh. "Trust me. Everybody wants to take care of me." She must have heard his disbelieving snort even though he tried to mask it with a cough. She glanced over her shoulder "You don't believe me?"

"Not exactly. I'm not sure I've ever met somebody who seems so capable of taking care of themselves as you. Or at least a person who gives little regard for anybody else's opinion."

Her eyes widened slightly. "That's really what you think of me?"

He nodded.

"Cool," she murmured as some of the joy he'd seen in her eyes minutes earlier seemed to return.

Carson was having trouble following their conversation, and he didn't think it had anything to do with the way Tessa's rosebud mouth distracted him. She was a bundle of contradictions. Brash and bold but somehow vulnerable and innocent at the same time. Bottom line: she was dangerous on many levels.

It was easy to forget that as she led him into the kitchen where Lauren sat at the kitchen table and the scent of garlic filled the air. The whole scene felt homey and normal. This was exactly the kind of feminine influence he knew his daughter needed and he couldn't possibly provide. Impossible because Tessa had already confirmed his suspicions that she wasn't a good role model for a young girl.

"Hey, Dad," Lauren said, her voice light and cheery when he'd expected censure because of the situation today.

"Hey, sweetheart. I'm sorry I got stuck in Portland. I promise it won't happen—"

"It's fine." She beamed at him. "I had so much

fun with Tessa. She helped me with my math homework, and she's way better at it than you."

"I'm great at math," he protested automatically.

"You're not much of a teacher." Lauren wrinkled her pert nose. "You're not patient. Tessa is patient, and she taught me how to crochet. Look, I've almost got a pot holder done."

"A pot holder?" Carson repeated feeling completely off-center. "This is what you guys did all afternoon?"

"We made dinner, too. Since we weren't sure when you were gonna be back. It's okay if my dad stays, too, right, Tessa?"

Carson didn't dare look at Tessa. She wouldn't want him staying for dinner. He'd been a complete jerk to her.

"Of course," she answered. To his surprise, there was no hesitation in her tone. What in the world was happening?

"Tessa said I can go with her to work this weekend."

There it was. Carson's doubts fell back into place. This was comfortable. "Absolutely not."

Lauren blinked as if he were speaking a different language "Why, though?"

Where to begin? "Because it's inappropriate for a kid to be—"

"Not my actual job," Tessa interrupted. "I volunteer at the retirement center on Saturdays. This week I'm teaching a class on felting."

Once again, Carson's brain scrambled for purchase. From what he thought he knew about her, he would have assumed felting to be some sort of newfangled sexual perversion, but she wouldn't be doing that at a retirement home. At least he hoped not.

While he was still playing mental catch-up, Tessa picked up something off the counter and lobbed it at him. Instinctually, he reached out and caught the small stuffed hedgehog-looking thing in his hands.

"We make felt animals," she explained like she knew exactly where his dirty mind had gone.

Who could blame him? It didn't make any sense that a woman like her would be volunteering. Hadn't she made it clear that her weekends were spent partying or flirting with men at the biker bar while she collected drink orders and tips in equal measure?

"Can I go, Dad?" Lauren's brow furrowed. "I'll get my homework and chores done first."

"We'll talk about it. But now we should get home."

"No," his daughter argued. "You said we could stay for dinner."

Right. He'd said that. But he hadn't meant it, especially when it felt like all of his preconceived notions were being waylaid.

"I just remembered that I have extra work to do."

Lauren frowned. "You always have work to do."

"That's not fair." He hated feeling the sting of her judgment. "I'm trying to—"

"I have work to do as well now that you mention it." Tessa moved toward the stove. "The pasta pie that Lauren so expertly assembled is ready, so I'll scoop out a serving for myself and I can send the big dish home with you. I don't do much with leftovers anyway."

"Thank you," Carson said quietly, still trying to wrap his mind around this new version of Tessa and to figure out if she was as big of a threat to Lauren as he wanted to believe.

In some ways he needed that to be true because it was a surefire excuse for staying away from her. And he knew without a doubt he needed to stay away from her.

Based on the ferocity with which his daughter packed her book bag, he could tell she wasn't happy. Join the club, he figured.

"Thank you again," he told Tessa when she wrapped the casserole dish in foil then put it in an insulated carrying case. "I'll return everything to you in the morning."

"It's fine. I'm glad I was able to help."

"I can pay you."

"That's offensive."

"I figured if you were desperate enough for money

that you'd work at the Thirsty Chicken, you could use a little extra income."

"I work there because I like it. I like your daughter, too." She shoved the carrying case at him. "Too bad I can't say the same for you."

Her temper made him smile. As much of a conundrum as she was, sweet or sassy she wouldn't take any grief from him. He respected her for that.

His chest pinched as she gave Lauren a warm hug and told her to FaceTime if she needed help finishing the pot holder.

"I'll see you on Saturday," his daughter said. "Don't forget me." Lauren turned to him. "You agreed."

"I'm not sure I did."

"Dad."

Somehow she made those three letters into two long syllables.

"Let's go. We'll talk more at home."

Tessa opened the front door and waved to his daughter. "Goodbye, Lauren. I'll see you soon."

He narrowed his eyes, but Tessa arched a brow and winked at him. She was dangerous, for sure but he still walked toward his truck with a smile on his face.

Chapter Four

Tessa tried—and probably failed—to hide her surprise as Carson approached her Jeep Saturday morning, following his daughter down the gravel driveway.

"Good morning," she said to Lauren as the girl climbed into the back seat. "I didn't realize your dad was coming with us."

"He started watching the felting videos on YouTube with me and got really into it," the girl reported. "Penguins are his favorite animals, so can we make penguins today?"

Tessa arched a brow as Carson climbed in next to her. She glanced at him out of the corner of her eye.

There was no way she trusted herself to look at him fully. "Penguins?"

"They're cute." He didn't crack a smile as he said the words.

She adjusted the volume on the radio as she backed out of the driveway.

"Cute my left foot," she said under her breath. "You don't trust me with your daughter."

He tapped a finger against his denim-clad leg but didn't answer. It shouldn't matter. The more people there to help with the class, the better. Her Saturday events at the retirement center were popular. Tessa liked the residents. She always had. Maybe it was so many years of sitting on the sidelines that made her more comfortable with older generations of people than she was with her own contemporaries.

She glanced at Lauren in the rearview mirror. "How did your social studies test go?"

"I got a little confused about the geography part," the girl admitted, "but I still got an A."

"I didn't know you had a social studies test this week," Carson said, his voice tight.

"I didn't need help studying or anything."

Tessa could feel Carson's steely gaze on her but kept her eyes trained on the road. "You knew?" he demanded quietly.

"Yep."

She wasn't about to tell him that his daughter had

shown up at her house after school on Thursday. The girl had a babysitter who stayed with her on the days she didn't go to the aftercare program and had told the woman she was going to visit a neighborhood friend. According to Lauren, the girl walked her to the end of the driveway but didn't question her further.

Tessa knew Carson wouldn't appreciate that she had been that friend.

Tessa liked it, though. She felt an odd connection to Lauren. The girl had shared her history with asthma and how it impacted her life. Tessa could relate.

Lauren continued to chatter about school and a new influencer she was following as Tessa drove down the mountain pass.

"How are you following influencers?" Carson asked. "You don't even have a phone."

"I have a tablet," Lauren reminded him.

"That's to use for homework."

"Dad, it's not a big deal. Half the girls in my class have real phones."

"They shouldn't."

"Tessa, tell him he's behind the times," Lauren pleaded. "I need a phone."

Tessa laughed softly at the intensity of the girl's tone.

"I agree with your dad, kiddo."

"You should enjoy being a kid and not worry about what's happening online."

"I can't even be a real kid. Everybody in my class plays soccer, and I'm no good at it. Plus I get out of breath too quick."

Tessa's heart ached for the girl. She knew all too well what it was like to struggle and feel like you had no chance of fitting in.

Tessa wondered what would have happened if her mother or anyone in her family had helped her believe that she could rise above her physical limitations. Would her difficult childhood actually have changed?

"You can do anything you want," she told Lauren as she pulled to a stop in the retirement village parking lot. "Don't let anybody make you believe you can't and that goes double for yourself."

She turned to look at Lauren. "If you want to learn soccer, do it. You can play soccer."

The girl didn't look entirely convinced, but her mouth softened slightly. "Maybe."

"Absolutely," Carson said. "We'll get a ball and start practicing this weekend."

"Really?" Lauren bit down on her lower lip. "You know they have practices at night and games on weekends?"

"Awesome." Carson nodded.

"Mommy said weekends are for families and

sleeping in. Soccer games are sometimes in the morning, Dad."

Tessa felt rather than saw the ripple of anger that went through Carson. "Your old man's an early bird, sweetheart. I'd love to go to a Saturday soccer game if my best girl was playing."

Tessa knew he meant it, and it softened her attitude toward him despite her better judgment. He might be a jerk to her, but that didn't mean she couldn't appreciate his dedication to his daughter.

Tessa greeted the woman at the reception desk as they walked into the retirement community. The place was set up with a wing for independent living as well as one for people who needed more assistance and a memory care unit. The receptionist was only a couple of years older than Tessa, and there was no missing the woman's approving perusal of Carson. Not that Tessa cared.

She could well imagine that being ogled was familiar territory to him and also none of her business. For his part, he was polite but not exactly encouraging, which Tessa appreciated more than she should. She introduced Lauren to the activities director, a man in his early fifties named Thomas who met them at the entrance to the dining hall.

"Everyone's excited," he told Tessa. "Your classes are a hit. And I appreciate you recruiting additional volunteers."

Lauren smiled broadly as he shook her hand.

"I'm not really volunteering," Carson said. "I'm more of a chaperone."

"I bet Tessa will get you involved," Thomas said with a laugh. "No one can resist her."

Tessa snorted then tried to cover it with a cough. Carson didn't glance at her, and she had to think it was on purpose.

"Let's go. We've got animals to felt."

They carried the supplies to the front of the room. The tables had been arranged so that everyone in a chair was facing her. She greeted the familiar faces and waved at some of the new participants.

She introduced herself and the craft for the day and then made a show of introducing Lauren as her very capable assistant.

The girl looked nervous to have so many eyes on her, but she smiled and waved.

"And we've got an extra special volunteer with us today," Tessa said, turning her smile toward Carson who'd slunk off to the back of the room. "Lauren's dad, Carson Campbell, is also here to help."

He raised his hands like a shield and shook his head.

"Oh, but I forgot…" Tessa said in a stage whisper. She leaned forward. "Carson is a bit shy. I'm sure you all will give him a warm Brookdale welcome."

Led by Thomas, the residents inside the dining

hall clapped and a couple of the feistier women let out enthusiastic catcalls.

Carson continued to shake his head, and Tessa continued to smile at him.

"Go help your dad," she said to Lauren. "He's bashful."

The girl laughed at that description but dutifully ran to the back of the room and tugged on her father's hand.

The applause got louder as he joined Tessa at the front.

"You don't play fair," he said under his breath.

"I can't believe you thought I would," she answered, making sure her smile didn't waver.

When the room went quiet she opened up her box of samples. "Everybody get excited. Our first animal will be a penguin."

Carson couldn't believe he'd spent the last two hours making felt animals and was even more shocked that he'd enjoyed it.

What the hell had his life become?

As he collected the final bits of leftover yarn from a table in the back of the Brookdale dining hall, Lauren ran up to him, threw her arms around his waist and gave him a full-on, half-a-minute hug.

"That was so much fun, Daddy. Can we go get the soccer ball now?"

Daddy.

His heart stuttered in his chest.

She hadn't called him that since before he'd picked her up from Delilah. Somehow he'd become plain old dad to his daughter, which shouldn't feel like an insult but somehow did. She was growing up. He understood, but ten still felt young.

Lauren was his baby, although she seemed to be past the age where a trip to the toy aisle or candy store could make up for all the ways he wasn't cutting it as a father.

Yet making a felt zoo had done the trick.

He needed to up his game.

"I think we should add an ice cream excursion along with sports equipment. I'm going to need some fuel before we practice our dribbling."

"Basketball players dribble," Tessa said as she joined them.

"Soccer players also dribble." Carson smiled as a look of abject confusion settled on Tessa's face.

"Really? I thought they kicked the ball."

"Yeah, Dad." Lauren turned so she was standing next to her new friend in a show of solidarity he couldn't help but appreciate. He knew that managing social landscapes with kids her own age didn't always come easily to his shy daughter.

"They kick the ball, yes, but it's called dribbling when you're controlling it to bring it down the field."

"Got it," Tessa said, nodding like she was truly committing his words to memory.

"Got it," Lauren echoed.

"I'm sure with your dad's help, you're going to be the best dribbler around in no time."

Lauren hugged him again then skipped off to collect her pile of felt animals from the demonstration table at the front of the room.

"I don't know what I did to deserve your faith in me," Carson told Tessa. "But I appreciate it."

"You're a good dad. A judgmental, grumpy, pain in the patoot for the most part, but a good dad."

He grinned. "I also appreciate the heartfelt compliment."

"Thanks for your help today." She appeared flustered that he'd thanked her instead of engaging in another round of verbal sparring.

"You didn't give me much choice."

"You still stepped up."

"What can I say? I'm a sucker for a penguin."

She laughed, and the sound reverberated through him like the trickle of water in a cool mountain stream on a hot summer day. Refreshing and light and able to make him feel like he wasn't messing things up quite as badly as he suspected.

"We're already looking forward to your next class," Thomas told Tessa as they walked to the front entrance. "I can't wait to see what you come up with."

Carson couldn't resist leaning closer to her when the front door closed behind them. "Have you told him about the cherry trick?"

She stumbled and possibly would have fallen flat on her face, but Carson shifted the container he carried to one arm and held her up with the other.

"Whoa, there," he whispered. She was plastered against him, her bright hair tickling his chin. It felt far too good to hold her, and it took him an extra few seconds before he forced himself to let go.

Her chest rose and fell in shallow puffs of air. At least he wasn't the only one affected.

She avoided his gaze and dug in her purse for the Jeep keys, unlocking the vehicle with the fob.

"Do you want to get ice cream with us?" Lauren asked as they approached the car. "Daddy said we could stop before we got the soccer ball. If we drive up the mountain to pick up his car it's going to take so long. Please, Tessa."

Tessa's mouth looked strained. "You and your dad might want some time on your own this afternoon."

"Nope. We get all kinds of time on our own. Right, Dad?"

Why hadn't he realized that being a parent was like death by a thousand paper cuts? He nodded. "We'd love to have you join us. It's the least I can do now that you've taught me the lifelong skill of animal felting."

Tessa's rosy lips twitched. "I guess it would take too long to get up and down from the cabin, and Main Street Perk has the best flavors."

"Yay," Lauren shouted then scrambled into the back of the Jeep.

How had he gone from warning Tessa Reynolds away from his daughter to willingly spending the day with her? She was different than he'd expected her to be. Even though he'd known that she volunteered on a regular basis at the retirement center, he hadn't expected her easy way with the residents.

Most of the women he'd dated or in Delilah's case, married, had been selfish with their time. Even when Delilah had gone to the obligatory military events, he'd always been able to sense the resentment that she was spending her time doing something other than exactly what she wanted to do.

A part of him had even wondered if Tessa volunteered for some self-serving reason, which is what he would have expected from Delilah.

The thought wasn't fair.

He wasn't being fair. In his heart, he knew that. He was taking his own experience and prejudice and putting it on to Tessa. All she'd done was give him a little bit of sass, tempt him beyond measure, and chosen a place of employment that he might not agree with. But it was none of his business to approve or disapprove of her choices.

Life had been simple in the military. At least for Carson. He'd excelled in the navy because he saw things in black and white. Being a full-time parent involved so much gray area, and he floundered when he had to maneuver through it. It was like slogging through a muddy swamp in the middle of a blizzard. Although in reality he knew snowstorms didn't happen in swampy areas, so it was just one more way he was discombobulated.

He wanted Tessa to fit into the black-and-white parts of his life. That seemed like the only way to overcome his attraction to her. To cast her as the bad guy—or in this case the bad girl.

He was the upstanding father who wanted people in his life who would be a good influence on his impressionable daughter.

A woman who stirred him to his very core couldn't possibly fit that mold because his penchant had always been for women who weren't the right choice for him.

He hadn't been with anybody more than on a casual basis since the end of his short-lived marriage. That had been an epic mistake, and his daughter was paying the price for it.

"Dad only likes strawberry," Lauren said from the back of the Jeep. "He won't even put sprinkles on it."

Tessa let out an exaggerated gasp. "No sprinkles? You really are a stick-in-the-mud."

He feigned irritation but her teasing amused him. "Strawberry is a classic flavor. The perfect texture and a great mix of sweet and tangy."

This time her soft inhalation didn't seem feigned. He glanced over and saw that color infused her cheeks. What had he said to garner that reaction? Sweet and tangy.

Heat pooled in his stomach. Innocent words but he understood the double meaning. Understood that they could just as easily describe Tessa. He could well imagine developing a penchant for her sort of flavor.

Chapter Five

"Tell us more about Carson and the ice cream," Ella urged the following evening as she poured a glass of wine for Tessa in the kitchen of the duplex she rented on the other side of Starlight.

"Did he slurp at it or do anything weird with his tongue?" Madison asked. "Because it's gross when people are loud lickers."

"I can't imagine Carson Campbell doing anything gross." Cory wiggled her eyebrows. "I'm not even sure you can use the word *gross* and a man that hot in the same sentence."

Tessa took a big swig of her wine, barely appreciating the flavor. She needed something to relax her. Normally a meeting of the Chop It Like It's Hot Cooking Club would be the highlight of her weekend.

She had met her friends when she responded to a flyer tacked up in the coffee shop advertising a cooking club several months earlier. Their first meeting had been at Trophy Room, and she'd discovered that Cory had bribed—or perhaps more accurately blackmailed—Madison into teaching her and whoever joined them the basics of cooking.

Ella had done it to impress a man and Cory was trying to prove to Jordan that she could fit into the Starlight community with or without his support. Tessa had come because she'd been new to town, and while she'd spent hours in front of her mirror perfecting a less buttoned-up look, she hadn't actually had the guts to wear makeup or the new clothes she'd bought anywhere but in her own house at the time.

She'd expected the meeting to be awkward because she could medal in awkward if it was an Olympic sport. They may have started out that way because all four women came from different backgrounds, and on the surface, didn't seem to have enough in common to become friends.

They'd become the best of friends, but her best friends could still annoy the heck out of her. "Eating ice cream isn't sexy," she said, earning a mix of blank stares and amused glances from her friends.

"Come on." Ella took a dainty bite of naan topped

with butter chicken. "Carson could recite the alphabet and it would be sexy. He's got that brooding military vibe going on."

Cory nodded. "Plus those aviator sunglasses. They are hot."

"He'd be even sexier reciting the alphabet naked." Madison chuckled to herself. "Or maybe we could get him to conjugate some verbs. I wonder if he speaks any other languages."

Tessa felt heat rise to her cheeks. "First, you shouldn't objectify a man, even a handsome one. Second, have you dated him?" she demanded of Madison. "You guys seemed pretty chummy the other day."

"I don't do chummy." The chef placed the lid on the pot and turned down the knob on the stove. Since that first meeting, they'd alternated hosting duties for the club.

Tessa had learned so much from Madison, although more often than not she still had cereal or a frozen dinner heated in the microwave for dinner.

It seemed sad and lonely to cook for just one.

Her mom was a great cook, although she'd insisted that Tessa eat a bland, healthy, boring diet. No acid, nothing spicy or processed or fried. So she'd make a meal for the rest of the family and a separate meal for Tessa. She knew her mother meant well but it only made her feel more divided from her family when she couldn't even enjoy the same food as them.

"He called you the other day when he needed help with his daughter," Tessa pointed out, trying to sound casual. She shouldn't care if Madison had something going with Carson. Neither of them was her business.

Cory waved a piece of bread at Tessa as she got up. "But you were the one to help him and now you're besties with his daughter. Ella, can I use your computer to pull up a site with new centerpiece ideas? Who wants to give their opinion?"

"No one," Madison said without hesitation.

"I'll go," Ella said. "But I'm taking the naan with me." She grabbed the basket.

Tessa could feel Madison studying her as the other two women moved toward the tiny office situated at the front of the duplex.

She glanced up. "What? I know you have something to say. Out with it."

Madison quirked a brow. "If I'm interested in Carson and you're getting close to Lauren, does that mean you're trying to skim my milk and take the man I want?"

Tessa thought about that for a moment. "Actually, I'm lactose intolerant."

Madison burst out laughing. "You're the best, Pollyanna."

"Why do you call me that?" Tessa asked softly. "I've made it very clear that I'm no innocent."

"That's right." Madison squeezed another lemon slice into the iced tea she was drinking. The woman loved iced tea with extra lemons. It was the only thing Tessa ever saw her drink. "You are a rebel."

"You don't believe me."

"Not one bit."

"Why? You only met me a couple of months ago. I shared plenty of stories about the trouble I've gotten into in my life."

"You're creative. I'll give you that. Although I think Rory Gilmore beat you to the punch on stealing the yacht. Season seven if I remember correctly?"

Tessa's mouth dropped open. She had indeed stolen that particular story from the popular television show. She liked Rory better when she'd thrown off the good girl mantle and embraced her inner rebel.

"I didn't make everything up."

"But most of it," Madison suggested. Not unkindly. "Trust me, I did a lot of stupid things back in my day. You don't have the look of somebody who's been around the block a time or two."

Frustration speared through Tessa. "How do I get it?" she couldn't help but ask.

Madison chuckled. "Trust me. You don't want it."

"I do. More than anything."

"Why?"

"I might not be a rebel, but I'm sick of being sheltered and innocent. I want to live on my terms. That's the whole reason I came to Starlight. Not so that I could trade towns but continue to live my same boring life."

"You're a lot of things," Madison told her. "Definitely a handful. But you're not boring. And even if you were, is boring so bad?"

"It's the worst," Tessa muttered.

"I came to Starlight for boring. That's all I want is boring." Madison tapped her fingernails on the granite countertop. "I would have killed to live the fairy-tale life I imagine you had before coming here."

"My life wasn't a fairy tale. It was a prison."

"'Why do you stay in prison when the door is so wide-open?'" Madison lifted a hand. "That's a Rumi quote by the way."

"I'm impressed, I think," Tessa murmured, "but I don't get how it relates to me."

"Think about it." Madison glanced over as Ella and Cory returned.

"What do you think about gold dresses?" Cory nodded vigorously like she could elicit their agreement that way.

"I don't think about gold dresses." Madison gave a mock shudder.

"I'll wear anything if it has a plunging neckline," Tessa said. She patted her breasts, which had been helped this evening by one of the padded bras she bought when she started work at the Thirsty Chicken. "If the girls are going to a wedding reception, they need to look their best." She flicked a glance at Madison that said she didn't get that line from a book of poetry or a television show.

Madison rolled her eyes while Cory and Ella stared at her blankly for a moment. She wondered if she was fooling anyone with her attitude. She wanted to believe they believed what she wanted them to. So she kept her eyes straight ahead. And popped a piece of naan into her mouth.

"Gold is going to look beautiful on all of you," Cory insisted.

Madison held up a hand. "Hold on. Why would we all be wearing matching dresses?"

"Because you're going to be my bridesmaids."

"Oh, heck no," Madison said, then let out a low whistle. "You do not want me in the wedding party."

"Of course I do."

"I thought I was going to be making the food."

Cory shook her head. "You are my friend. Not paid staff at my wedding."

Tessa felt rather than saw the change in Madison. It was a softening of her normally rock-hard shell.

Tessa had never given much thought to the life experiences of healthy people. She was so much a part of the community who had suffered childhood illness. In her mind, anyone who hadn't had to deal with regular hospital visits or the constant worry if an organ was going to continue functioning had it easy.

That had been naive and unfair, she was coming to realize.

She didn't know what exactly Madison had dealt with in her life but her past had left scars. Maybe not visible ones like the crisscross of puckered skin on Tessa's belly, but scars that covered damage just the same.

She would think about the Rumi quote. She wasn't ready to give up the new her she was trying to create. But she would at least consider that there might be other options.

Bright and early Monday morning, Carson headed down the mountain pass with Lauren babbling happily to him from the back seat.

His daughter had been in a sunny mood since their visit to the retirement community and the subsequent trip to the ice cream store and purchase of a soccer ball.

He hated to admit that he owed his tempting neighbor a debt of thanks, but the fact couldn't be denied. The felt zoo Lauren had created went with her everywhere. The menagerie ate dinner with them and stood watching over her when she took her evening bath and then received a prominent place on her pillow each night.

She'd even started talking to him as if she were the animals and it was as if they gave her the courage to speak more freely than she'd been willing to up until now.

Pete the penguin had no problem telling him about how he was too strict on screen time rules, while Harriett the hedgehog often lamented being the new animal in their little crew and how difficult it was to make friends with people who'd grown up together.

Carson hadn't bothered to point out that all of the animals had been created within the same two-hour time span. Instead, he'd responded as if the questions and comments were really coming from Lauren's zoo. His daughter had almost visibly relaxed once she realized he intended to play along, and Lauren became more animated and cheerful overall.

Carson had taken his cue from her and spent the remainder of the weekend feeling more positive than he had in ages, at least until he'd received an email from Delilah late last night.

Things are great in Europe. I even got to meet Prince William's second cousin at an event. He has a kid Lauren's age. Wouldn't it be awesome if my girl ended up married to royalty?

By the time Carson finished the rambling email, his blood had been boiling. Potential matchmaking aside, his ex-wife hadn't asked about their daughter or given her any sort of personal message within the email. It felt more like reading a middle school diary entry than communication from a parent who hadn't seen her child in months.

He didn't share any of that with Lauren. His daughter had lost enough and he didn't want to add to the rejection he knew she must feel.

Instead, over breakfast he told her a bit about what her mom was doing, leaving out the part about marrying her off to some random royal. But he'd added that Delilah asked about her and expressed how much she missed her daughter. It was a testament to Lauren's mood that she hadn't questioned him. A week earlier when she'd asked why her mom never called, he'd offered some lame excuse about the time zone and her hectic schedule.

His daughter obviously had believed that lie but this morning, she'd simply sighed and then negotiated an argument between Pete and Harriett.

As he drove toward the curve that led to the turnoff to town, he noticed a familiar red Jeep pulled to the side of the shoulder.

"It's Tessa," Lauren said from the back seat. "Daddy, it's Tessa. You have to stop."

"I'll stop." He would have stopped without Lauren urging him to and wondered what he'd done to deserve his daughter's lack of faith.

"Can I get out, too?"

"It's not safe, baby girl. You stay here and I'll see what's going on."

"I'm fine," Tessa said before he had a chance to greet her.

"How's the wild-woman mobile?"

She gave him a funny look. "Not as good," she said sullenly. "I think it's the carburetor. They warned me about it at the last service appointment, but I haven't had time to get it in."

"Too busy with all those thirsty chickens?"

Her eyes narrowed, and he immediately held up his hands. "Sorry. I wasn't trying to be a jerk."

"But it comes so naturally to you," she answered.

"Okay, I deserved that. How can I help?"

"You can't. I've already called a tow truck."

"I'm taking Lauren to school. Why don't I give you a lift into town and they can pick up your car later?"

"I wasn't going to town. I'm on my way to Seattle. I have a work meeting there, so unless you've got some sort of magical powers, there's not much you can do for me."

"Daddy has a plane," Lauren said as she bounced up behind him.

"I thought I told you to stay in the car."

"You were taking too long, and there were no other cars around. His plane is like magic," Lauren explained. "It's way faster than driving. We went to Seattle last month 'cause I wanted to go to the top of the needler."

"The Space Needle," Carson corrected gently.

"Yep," his daughter agreed. "So you'll take Tessa with you today? Right, Daddy? Maybe I can skip school and go?"

"No skipping school," Carson said at the same time as Tessa, which surprised him. He would have pegged her for a fan of truancy.

"I'm sure Tessa doesn't want to fly to Seattle with me this morning."

"You're absolutely right." Tessa nodded then chewed on her bottom lip. "I also really need to get to Seattle this morning. I have a meeting with my boss."

Carson let out a little snort. "Is that so?"

He watched as her shoulders stiffened. "It is. The meeting is for my day job."

Had he known she had another job? He didn't think so. Because he'd spent way too much time picturing her sleeping in until noon and then watching daytime soap operas as she recovered from whatever she'd done the night before.

God, he really was a judgmental jerk, just like she'd accused.

"But I don't want to go with you," she added.

"You don't have to be scared," Lauren offered, taking Tessa's hand. "Daddy's a really good pilot."

Daddy. She kept using that word. His daughter could play him like a violin.

"I need to get her to school." Carson let his eyes drift closed for a moment. "I'm heading to the airfield from there. It's a thirty-minute trip into the city and I have a couple of hours' worth of work to do once I get there. You're welcome to come with me but I'm not going to force you."

"Okay."

"Seriously?"

"It's a really important meeting."

"I made a dress for Harriet Hedgehog out of an old washcloth," Lauren said as she tugged Tessa forward. "It's in the truck."

"I can't wait to see it," Tessa answered. She followed his daughter without hesitation. Then she paused and glanced over her shoulder. "Is it okay if we drop off my keys to the mechanic on the way out of town? That will mean they can get started on the car immediately."

Carson forced himself to swallow back the rising feeling of panic filling his chest like a surging stream. "Sure," he agreed.

The cockpit of his plane was tiny. He figured he could manage not to touch her during the flight but she would fill the interior with her scent and there wouldn't be a damn thing he could do to stop it. Lord help him get through this day.

Chapter Six

"Are you ready to talk?"

Julia Reynolds, Tessa's older sister, said the words calmly as if she hadn't been barking orders at Tessa for the past two hours.

Tessa kept her expression neutral. "We've been talking, Juls." She lifted the notebook she'd been furiously scribbling tasks into. "I have five pages of notes to confirm that."

"You know what I mean. When are you coming home?"

"Is there something about my performance on the job that has suffered since I moved to Starlight?

I thought we agreed with how much you're on the road, it doesn't matter where I'm located."

Julia studied her for a weighted moment. They shared the same crystal-blue eyes but Julia's hair was a rich mahogany color, something Tessa had coveted since she'd stuck out in class as a skinny, pale, flame-haired kid. Her sister's beauty was understated but undeniable. She was seven years older, an independent teenager by the time Tessa was old enough to remember her. She'd become a psychologist who worked with patients with chronic illness and pain.

Then six years ago, Julia had written a runaway best seller about overcoming obstacles and using mental tools to manage physical challenges. At first, Tessa had been irritated that her sister had mined Tessa's personal struggles to advance her own career. In some ways, she knew she owed Julia for sucking up so much of the attention in their family.

Once Tessa's health issues started, her parents—and particularly their mother—had become obsessed with keeping her well.

Julia was healthy, smart and self-sufficient, so she'd largely been left to fend for herself. Was it any wonder that Tessa's experience had influenced her sister in a profound way? Her illness had engulfed their entire family and been almost as devastating for Julia as it was to Tessa.

Julia had been the first person to be tested to determine if she was a match for Tessa when it became clear that a new kidney was the only option. She hadn't been a match, but their father had. Randy Reynolds had gone through a battery of mental and physical testing in order to be approved to donate an organ to his younger daughter. It was a gift Tessa could never repay, although he assured her he would have done it a thousand times over if he could.

But the way the transplant bound her to her father had changed something in the dynamic between her and Julia. She wondered what Julia's legions of followers and readers would think about Dr. J's lingering resentment and the shadow Tessa's illness had cast over all of their lives.

"It matters to Mom," Julia said after a moment.

Tessa nodded. "She put you up to this?"

"She went as far as to suggest I threaten to fire you if you wouldn't agree to move back."

"I think there's the hook for your next best seller," Tessa commented with a wink, trying to sound like she wasn't gutted that her mom didn't believe in her ability to manage on her own in the big, wide world.

It had always been this way. For most of her life, Tessa had gone along with it. She'd been too sick to fight. But she was healthy now. Yes, she needed to take care of herself and she did. She took her autoimmune medicine and monitored her health religiously. She had a green smoothie every morning for breakfast and followed it up with a diet that would make her nutritionist proud.

She was thrilled to be on her own and to be able to breathe without someone always hovering, but she often felt like she was only pretending to be normal.

Still, she wasn't going home. "Are you going to fire me? Because even that kind of threat won't make me change my mind. And I'm not sure how your die-hard fans would react to the benevolent Dr. J canning her disabled sister as a manipulation tactic."

Julia released a harsh breath. "Little Tessa is showing her teeth," she murmured. "You've changed, and I'm not just talking about your unfortunate fashion and makeup choices."

"My prerogative," Tessa muttered, realizing she sounded like a petulant child.

Julia inclined her head as she ran a hand through her thick, mahogany hair. Her blue eyes seemed to see too much of Tessa. She'd been a swimmer in high school and still held one of their high school's distance records. Basically the opposite of Tessa in every way.

Julia was a good person. Tessa knew she was dedicated to her work and to the fans who put her on a pedestal. Tessa had been one of those people for most of her life. Julia was the person she'd most wanted to emulate.

She'd imagined waking up one day with her health

problems gone and a chance to live the life her defective kidney prevented her from living. She would have even been happy with her red hair if she'd been healthy. When that had finally happened, her mother hadn't been able to release the chronically ill version of Tessa. It felt as though moving away was the only option for truly embracing the life she wanted.

"You even got your ears double pierced," Julia said as if that was something scandalous. "Tell me you don't have a tattoo."

"No, but if I wanted to get one, I would."

"Good for you," Julia said after another moment. "I'm not going to fire you, Tessa. And not because I'm worried about your health. I like working with you. Heck, you keep me sane most days. I have colleagues who would poach you in a heartbeat. Trust me. I understand how lucky I am to have you managing my career."

"Then why are you asking me when I'm going to move back?"

"Because it's the only way I can think of to get Mom off my case." Julia grabbed a can of alcoholic soda water from the hotel room's minibar.

Her sister was based in Cleveland but traveled extensively between book tours and guest appearances on talk shows, both on the national and regional stage. She was in Seattle to deliver a keynote for a multinational computer company's annual meeting.

It wasn't the sort of speaking engagement she normally accepted. Tessa assumed their mother had put her up to it so she could get eyes on Tessa in person and make sure she was okay.

Her mom would never believe she was doing great.

"As usual, I'm bringing you down." Tessa didn't usually allow herself to wallow in self-pity but every once in a while she succumbed to the urge.

Julia popped open the can of seltzer and took a long drink. "Don't make me go through the five stages with you."

Tessa chuckled. The five stages of mindful manifestation were the basis of Julia's system for moving on and overcoming challenges. Tessa had come up with the first three herself after a long stay in the hospital when she was in tenth grade.

When Julia's career had taken off and she'd needed someone to manage her calendar and her speaking engagements, as well as edit and organize her book material, she'd hired Tessa. At that point, Tessa had graduated from college but her kidney had stopped functioning to the point that between dialysis and her general lack of energy, she was barely able to leave the house.

She knew her sister had given her the job out of pity and love, which were so mixed up in Tessa's mind that it was hard for her to tell the difference.

It turned out she was fantastic as a virtual assistant. Even when she felt the worst, having a reason to get up every day and slog through her to-do list helped her cope.

Yes, she owed Julia for hijacking their parents' attention and for the chance at a career, but her sister had to be lying when she said Tessa was a partner in her career. Tessa was unable to believe she could be that valuable to anyone.

"I like my life in Starlight," she said. "Nobody there remembers me as this sickly little kid who used to visit Aunt Marsha."

"Is that why you're dressing like some teenybopper Insta model?"

Tessa laughed softly. "Leave the social media to me, Juls. But yeah. I'm trying some new things. I want to figure out who I am when my identity isn't wrapped up in being sick."

"Good for you."

"You don't mean that. You like me as the weak, helpless person who needs your charity."

Julia placed a hand to her heart. "Ouch. Don't sugarcoat it. Tell me what you really think."

"You aren't denying it."

Julia's brow furrowed. "I'm processing. It's what I do. I don't want you to feel helpless or like a charity case, Tessa. I don't think Mom wants that either. I'll admit we've gotten into a bad pattern in our family, but I've always admired you. I never thought you were weak. You went through too much without complaint."

"I complain plenty."

"Not really." Julia took another sip of her drink. "I've worked with a lot of chronically ill people and met even more at the various events around the country. You're strong, Tessa. Not because you got your ears pierced again or wear a whole bunch of goop on your face. You're strong because of who you are on the inside."

Emotion clogged Tessa's throat, and she swallowed it back. She wanted to believe she was strong. But her sister's words were vaguely reminiscent of Madison's cryptic advice about staying in prison. As if she were responsible for not being able to move on with her life as this healthy version of herself.

"Travel with me," Julia said suddenly.

Tessa felt her mouth drop open. "What?"

"On the tour." Julia leaned forward, her eyes bright. "You're the one who booked me at all these speaking engagements and interviews at so many media outlets. I'm going to be on the road through the summer. Let me get to know this new you."

"I can't." Tessa said the words automatically.

"Why?"

"I have a life in Starlight."

"Come on. You know Aunt Marsha would let you

out of the lease. It will be fun. You could talk to people at some of the meet and greets."

"Me? Why would anyone want to talk to me?"

"Because you're an inspiration."

"You're the one who writes the books and says all the quotable words. I just organize the calendar."

"You've lived this. You're the survivor."

"I just want to be normal and forget that any of that happened."

"What you've dealt with has shaped you into the person you are. Maybe it's time you start using that to help others. You might find there are other ways to change your life than with a new wardrobe."

"Don't Dr. J me. The thing about living my life is that I get to do it how I want. If that means black eyeliner then I'm going to go with it."

"Fine."

"Are you sure you aren't asking me so you can keep watch over me and report back to Mom? Make sure I'm taking my meds and not pushing myself too hard?"

Julia drained the last of her seltzer and then leveled Tessa with a look of disappointment so intense it made Tessa's skin feel two sizes too small for her body. She hadn't meant to hurt her sister. "I thought we could start again. But I understand it's your journey. Try to remember you're not alone."

Tessa hadn't felt truly alone since coming to Starlight and meeting her friends. She'd always blamed her family for the distance that seemed to creep up between them. As if caring for her felt more like it was holding her captive. She thought about Madison's poetry quote once more but not for too long. She didn't want to consider that she might be to blame for the parts of her life she didn't like. It was easier to think she held no culpability.

"I appreciate the offer. I do want to get to know you in a different way, Juls." She wiggled her brows. "I've got a little more time before I need to meet my ride. Want to go get your ears double pierced?"

Julia chuckled. "Not this time, sis. Do you have to go back today? I'm going to be here until tomorrow morning. We could go out to dinner and you could spend the night. It's been a while since we had a sleepover."

"I don't have my car in the city," Tessa admitted.

The look of concern on her sister's face made her regret it. "What happened to your car? How did you get here? Tell me you didn't hitchhike."

"I'm wearing makeup which doesn't mean I'm going to be reckless." Tessa tried for patience as she spoke but wasn't sure she managed it. "I'm not stupid. I had some trouble with my car this morning. Routine stuff. My neighbor is a pilot and he was coming to the city so I bummed a ride with him."

"On one of those tiny planes? Tessa you…" Julia

bit down on her lower lip and nodded. "I'm glad you were still able to make it. I'm sure you were extremely safe with this neighbor."

The flight had been uneventful but as far as being safe with Carson, Tessa knew that was far from the truth.

Tessa walked into the restaurant that sat catty-corner to the Pike Place Market an hour later. Carson had texted her that he was grabbing lunch and the address of where to meet him.

She was keyed up from talking to her sister and everything that conversation had forced her to consider. A few months ago, she would have jumped at the opportunity to travel with Julia. Tessa yearned for adventure in any way she could get it. She knew it said a lot about how far she'd come that Julia had made the offer.

Dr. J wouldn't have considered it when Tessa was in Cleveland, no matter how much Tessa tried to convince her family that she could handle a regular life.

They didn't seem to care that the success rate after a kidney transplant with a living-donor organ was reported as 86 percent at five years and the average lifespan of a transplanted kidney was twelve to fifteen years. The future could be thought of as uncertain but she figured that was the truth for everyone. She was done letting her fears or limitations rule the day.

The restaurant smelled like fresh baked bread and rich chowder. She wished she had longer in Seattle to explore the city. Maybe she should consider Julia's offer. It wasn't as if there was anything truly keeping her tied to Starlight.

She glanced around the restaurant and saw Carson at a table in the back. He wasn't alone. A woman in a slim black pencil skirt and fitted T-shirt with the restaurant's logo emblazoned across the front rested her hip on his table and leaned into him.

Carson seemed to be shrinking back. She knew he hadn't dated anyone since coming to Starlight. Madison had been happy to share that tidbit with her. She got the impression he was far too consumed with getting a handle on single parenting to worry about romance, although it was just as clear from the tableau in front of her that he probably didn't lack offers from eager members of the opposite sex.

His personal business was none of Tessa's. She knew that on a rational level. That didn't mean watching some random woman put the moves on him sat well with her. She thought about the conversation with her sister. Julia might not think she needed makeup or new clothes to change her identity, but they certainly helped.

So much that Tessa found the nerve to grab a few

flowers from a vase sitting on the hostess desk. She ignored the fact that they were dripping on the polished wood floor as she made her way through the restaurant.

She fluffed her hair, yanked on her shirt to try to show a bit of cleavage—thank you again, padded bra—and did her best to swing her hips as she walked.

Awareness rippled across her skin the moment Carson noticed her. His gray eyes darkened and his mouth quirked at one corner as their gazes locked.

The heat in his expression made her stumble a step. Had a man ever looked at her that way? She didn't think so and wondered if she imagined what she saw in Carson's eyes. But that didn't change how she felt in the moment. She felt brave.

"I got these for you," she said as she arrived at the table.

"Pick them yourself?" he asked, glancing at the wet stems.

"Excuse me," the woman said, giving Tessa major stink eye. "We're having a private conversation here."

"Oh, this is important." Tessa offered the woman her best conspiratorial smile. "These are get-well flowers." She held up the makeshift bouquet and jostled them in the woman's face. "He's actually not supposed to be close to anyone until the infection clears up."

She heard Carson sputter out a laugh.

"Infection?" The woman looked confused.

Tessa nodded. "It's kind of private in nature, so we're not going to talk about it in great detail. But you might want to back up a few steps. For your own health."

The woman blinked then straightened from the table. She seemed to be working out something in her head. "This is a joke, right? You're just another one of his admirers."

Tessa smiled and leaned in like she was imparting a great secret. "I admire certain parts of him more than others." She dropped her voice to a whisper. "Unfortunately, that means I'm dealing with the same infection."

Before she could gauge the woman's reaction, her nose started to itch. She glanced at the cluster of flowers, which she realized contained daisies. Do not sneeze, she inwardly commanded herself but lifted her elbow to cover her mouth just as a giant sneeze erupted.

Carson's new friend yelped and jumped back, "You sneezed on me," she said on the hiss of breath. "That's disgusting."

"Yeah, lots of germs. But probably not the worst thing I could share with you right now."

The woman let out an outraged gasp then stalked toward the restaurant's kitchen.

"Hope I didn't interrupt anything important." Tessa slid into the chair across from Carson. She placed the flowers on the table between them.

"You rescued me." He flashed a wide smile and reached out a long finger to touch one of the colorful petals. "Although I'm not sure which drove her off faster, the insinuation about my diseased self or you snotting all over her."

Tessa wrinkled her nose. The believability of her as the other woman was somewhat tempered by the sneeze and the fact that her eyes were currently watering profusely and she could feel them getting puffier by the second.

"I should have checked the flowers. I'm allergic to daisies."

Carson stood and grabbed the stems from the table. She watched, along with several other women in the restaurant, as he moved to the hostess stand and placed them back in the vase.

He said something to the young woman working there that made her smile and nod. How could a man who was so surly with Tessa be completely charming with practically every other female he encountered? He returned to the table at the same time the waiter arrived.

"Can I get you something, miss ?" he asked Tessa. She eyed Carson's empty plate.

"You probably want to head back to Starlight?"

She could imagine he'd want to spend as little extra time with her as possible, especially after she'd all but made a spectacle of herself.

He shrugged. "Are you hungry?"

For so much more than she could name.

"A little," she answered as her stomach rumbled, loud enough that even the waiter snickered.

"She'll order," Carson told the young man.

"Clam chowder in a bread bowl," she said immediately.

"Anything to drink?"

"A Shirley Temple, please."

Tessa cringed as the waiter walked away. She'd placed her normal drink order without thinking and now embarrassment colored her cheeks. A grown woman who ordered a kiddie drink. Carson must think her ridiculous.

"I need the soda to settle my stomach," she told him like it was no big deal. She was the queen of faking it. "Normally, I'd stick with a beer but you don't want me puking all over your plane."

"Indeed I don't." He didn't smile but she caught the amusement in his tone. "Thanks for making this trip way more entertaining than it should have been, Red. Always an adventure with you."

Tessa felt her smile widen. She wasn't sure whether Carson meant the words as a compliment, but they filled her heart just the same.

Chapter Seven

Carson landed the plane at the regional airport just outside of Starlight later that afternoon. A glance to the right showed his passenger still fast asleep.

The meeting with her sister had clearly been a whopper. He could barely believe it when Tessa had told him about her day job. Personal assistant to the famous Dr. J, who also happened to be her older sister.

He didn't follow much in the world of personal development or pop psychology, but Julia Reynolds was practically a household name. Tessa hadn't wanted to talk about her family or her work for Julia other than the basics of her duties.

As she'd sipped the silly drink she'd ordered at the restaurant, he almost wished he hadn't asked her. Her mood had gone from light and flirty to somber, as if the time she'd spent with her sister had covered her light with a heavy blanket. She hadn't even appreciated his joke about the cherry bobbing in her glass.

There were far more facets to Tessa than Carson wanted to admit, and every one of them fascinated him. She wouldn't be boxed in by any of his preconceived notions or clichéd beliefs.

She'd sashayed into the restaurant with her little performance, amusing the hell out of him. But there had also been an air of protectiveness toward him that made his heart tighten. Carson didn't need to be rescued by anyone but appreciated it just the same.

He was used to attention from women and got tired of turning them down. It had been nice to have Tessa take care of his unwanted admirer even if her sneeze had been more effective than her story about his so-called infection.

Who was Tessa Reynolds at her core? Carson didn't like the mystery of her even though she intrigued him on so many levels. No matter his growing attraction, his priority remained Lauren and her well-being. He didn't know how to trust Tessa when it came to his daughter. Was there a way to separate what he needed to do as a father from what he wanted as a man? He hadn't wanted anyone in a long time the way he desired Tessa. The intensity of it scared him. But how long would he be able to deny acting on it?

He pulled the plane to a stop in his normal parking space, planning to walk to his truck and drive it over so he could load the supplies he'd picked up in the city. It had taken months of hard work and making connections with business owners to carve out his niche in the region, and he appreciated being able to create his own schedule so that he could devote the time he needed to his daughter.

Tessa stirred as a gust of cold air entered the cabin. Spring in the Cascades was a fickle mistress. One day the whole mountain could be in bloom with the scent of blossoms and pine filling the air. On a dime, the weather would change with winter unwilling to give up its hold on the world.

His friend who'd recommended him for the pilot job had warned him that they could get snow as late as the first part of June. Carson appreciated Mother Nature keeping him on his toes. He'd learned a great deal of respect for the elements during his time in the military.

"I should have brought a jacket," Tessa said, wrapping her arms around herself. "Sorry I fell asleep. I think it's the copilot's job to keep the pilot awake, and I failed miserably."

"It's fine." Carson reached behind the seat and

handed her an old navy sweatshirt. "You can put this on. I'm going to bring the truck over and load it up."

"I'll help. Just give me a minute to wake up. I'm not exactly a rise and shiner."

His mouth went dry as the sudden image of her waking after a long night in his bed filled his brain. She would be warm and tousled, much like she appeared at the moment. Her dark eyeliner was smudged underneath those big eyes. He wondered, not for the first time, why she wore so much makeup. She certainly didn't need it. But her beauty choices were not his concern. Neither was thinking about how she would look when she woke.

He hopped down from the plane. "Take your time." *Keep your mind on the job*, he counseled himself as he walked across the airfield. She'd bummed a ride with him because she needed one, not to voluntarily spend more time with him.

It only took a few minutes to bring the truck around, but she already had most of the supplies in neat piles on the ground.

"Thanks. I'll get the rest. Some of the boxes are heavy."

"I'm strong." She lifted her arms as if to display her bicep muscles which were all but invisible under the bulk of his sweatshirt. He liked seeing her in his clothes. Far too much. They made quick work of the cargo and then headed toward town.

"Frank at the mechanic left me a message," Tessa told him after dialing her voice mail. "My car is ready."

Carson checked his watch. "Are you okay if we pick up Lauren on the way? She's in the school's aftercare program until five."

"Sure. I can even slink down in the front seat if you want me to."

He looked at her, once again baffled by the words that came out of her mouth. "Why would you need to do that?"

"So you don't start any rumors at the school. I'm sure those moms are always sniffing around for the latest scoop. You don't want to be part of it, although I bet you're a common topic of conversation."

"Why would they talk about me?"

"Because you're a hot single dad."

Carson couldn't help his smile. "Do you think I'm hot?"

Tessa looked at him like he had five heads. "My opinion has nothing to do with it. You are, in fact, physically perfect. How many times when you eat at a restaurant by yourself do you get approached by women?"

He felt his neck heat. "Sometimes."

"Rough percentage," she demanded.

"More than fifty."

She pointed at him. "You're lying. It's probably more than ninety."

"Close to one hundred," he said quietly.

She laughed, a hearty cackle that reverberated through him. "I'm curious." She raised a brow and tapped one finger on that rosebud mouth. "Is it mainly other customers or is it a combination of waitresses and random women who just catch a glimpse of you and lose all self-control?"

He rolled his eyes. "Now you're just being rude."

"Once again," she told him, "you aren't denying it."

"It's not like I ask for the attention."

"Right. And I feel so sorry for you and the fact that your perfect body and smoldering gaze makes women fall at your feet."

"You must be familiar with attention. The guy I was sitting next to at the Thirsty Chicken told me that nearly every customer there had tried to make a move on you."

She was silent for a moment, and he glanced over to find her staring at him with a confused expression. "Nobody makes moves on me." She said the words like they were fact, which he found hard to believe.

He saw the moment she realized that she'd owned something she shouldn't have and shook her head.

"I mean, I'm the one who makes the moves and I choose who I'm going to date…" She drew in a shallow breath. "Or, you know, just hook up with for the night."

"You're into random hookups?"

"Isn't everybody?" she asked on a rush of breath.

"I'm not."

"Well, that's too bad for you. Because I'm great at sex, so if we hooked up it would be the best night of your life."

He did his best not to yank the wheel, jam on the brakes, pull to the side of the road, and beg her to prove it.

He had a daughter to pick up from school and hadn't been joking when he told Tessa he didn't do hookups. Or one-night stands. Or anything remotely naked other than solo showering since he'd become a full-time single dad.

Instead he continued driving and tried to ignore the chemistry radiating between them. The interior of his truck was like a damn science experiment at the moment, and Carson—unfortunately—had always loved science.

"What exactly is it about Carson that gives you verbal diarrhea?"

Cory laughed as she asked the question, but it was the regrettable truth. It had been three days since their trip to Seattle and the unfortunate ride home in his truck where Tessa had blathered on about her sexual prowess.

A subject that was inappropriate on a good day but even more so for her because, and not even her best friends in Starlight knew, at age twenty-seven she was an actual virgin.

Tessa had never had a boyfriend, and despite her claims to the contrary, didn't partake in hookups. She'd spent most of her teenage years in and out of the hospital, and no one at her high school would have wanted to take on the charity-case sick girl in a relationship. Her life wasn't some sort of young adult movie after all.

Even if they had, Tessa hated her body. The road map written across it that told the story of everything she'd been through. Scars might be sexy on men who wore leather jackets and got into bar fights, but they weren't on young women. She knew that thanks to the darkness of that first night when she'd emerged from the hot springs—along with Carson's shock— he hadn't registered the details of her body, but that wouldn't happen again.

Maybe that's why she had made such a fool of herself in front of Carson with her claims. She wasn't exactly embarrassed by her inexperience, but it seemed to overshadow what she wanted from her life. She couldn't separate who she was now from who she'd been. She might not be the star of some teenybopper coming-of-age movie, but Tessa had watched enough of them to know that bad girls weren't virgins.

"He just pushes my buttons," she told Cory.

"Bush," Ben, Cory's toddler son repeated. Tessa had come to her friend's house after she'd finished her work with Julia today because Jordan was pulling a late night at Trophy Room and she needed some company. Cory was working on wedding centerpieces and Tessa had offered to help. They were making paper flowers and tying ribbon around the mason jars that would adorn each table.

Just like at the retirement center, she genuinely liked doing crafts. Really, she wasn't cut out to be a bad girl at all and almost regretted starting down the path of trying to prove to everyone, including herself, that she was.

"I'm just going to avoid him for the rest of my life."

"That's one option," Cory said with a smile. "However, don't you think that's going to be harder than necessary when you have to drive by his house to get to yours and his daughter clearly adores you?"

"She doesn't adore me. She's desperate for female attention."

"Have you found out any more details about his ex-wife? I asked Jordan, but he said Carson doesn't like to speak about it. You know how guys can be."

Tessa didn't really know how guys could be because she had little experience with them. "No, but I'm curious. Everything I know has come from Lauren, and she just says her mom is on tour with the new husband. I guess he's some sort of musician."

Cory ran a hand over Ben's downy hair. The boy didn't react, just continued to play with his blocks as if the loving touch from his mom was so natural he didn't even need to acknowledge it. "I can't imagine leaving Ben at any age for an extended period. Jordan and I have trouble scheduling a date night, let alone something more."

"If you ever need help, I'm available," Tessa told her friend. "It's not like I have much else going on."

"I appreciate that." Cory sighed. "Even with planning a small wedding, there's so much to do. I'm not sure where I'd fit in a night out, but I know it's important. Jordan's mom is going to keep him when we go on our honeymoon, which will be a huge gift."

She cleared her throat. "Speaking of your schedule, Jordan had a guy come into the bar a few nights ago who normally frequents the Thirsty Chicken over in Montrose. He mentioned a waitress named Tessa who works over there but lives in Starlight. I guess he was wondering why she wouldn't try to get a job closer to home."

Tessa continued to concentrate on the centerpieces even though it felt like her fingers weren't working properly. She could feel a blush creeping up her cheeks and, once again, cursed her fair complexion.

"I only work there once or twice a week," she said. No point in denying it. "Gosh, those bikers gossip like little schoolgirls."

"Do you need money?" Cory asked gently. "Because we can help—"

"No. I don't do it for the money. I just wanted to try it."

Cory frowned. "One of your life goals has been to work in a biker bar?" She sounded dubious.

"I wanted to go to a biker bar. That's how it started. You know I have my fresh-start bucket list."

"Right," Cory agreed, "but I would think it might include more things like travel to the Amalfi Coast or see the Eiffel Tower."

"I'd like to do those things. I'd like to do all the things. I haven't even been able to think that big yet. When we were little, there was this bar outside of Cleveland. We drove by it on the way to my grandma's house. It was actually way seedier than the Thirsty Chicken, if I'm being honest. My mom would freak out and make sure the doors of the car were locked as if the people smoking outside on the patio were going to rush over and try to ambush us as we rolled by. I spent so much of my life being protected. There are random things that represent something to me."

"Micro-rebellions."

Tessa liked the description. "Yeah, maybe that's it. I don't think my mom would have a problem with me traveling to Paris, but she'd lay an egg herself if she knew I was working in a bar like that."

"And that's important to you?"

"It always seemed important to me." Now Tessa wasn't sure what her priorities were. Her bad-girl bucket list was starting to seem silly. "You've always been able to take care of yourself. You and Ella and Madison. You're all naturally fierce. I'm still trying to learn how that works."

Cory lifted Ben onto her lap when the boy began to fuss. "I wasn't fierce or strong. I made a lot of dumb choices and made myself small for the guy I dated all through college. Having Ben gave me my strength."

"Are you suggesting that getting pregnant would be better than working at the Thirsty Chicken?"

"Definitely not. My point is it's not what you do. It's who you are that gives you strength. I found mine through being a mom. If I thought about it, that strength was inside me all the time. I just didn't know how to tap into it."

Panic and hope welled together inside of Tessa.

She didn't want her emotions to rule her life, just like she didn't want fear to win the day. She blinked rapidly then smiled at her friend. "It sounds like I need to get the personal identity version of ruby slippers and click my heels. You make a pretty stellar Good Witch, Cory."

"I'm here to grant your wishes, whenever you need it."

As much as Tessa appreciated that, she knew she had to find the strength Cory talked about on her own. She simply wasn't convinced she had it in her.

Chapter Eight

Carson sat in his darkened truck late Friday night and stared at the entrance to the Thirsty Chicken. He knew Tessa was inside because her Jeep with the "All Good Vibes" sticker on the back window was parked on the far side of the bar.

He wanted to talk to her about that, to tell her she needed to park closer to the building where her vehicle would be flooded in light whenever she left. He wanted to ask if she had somebody walk her out after last call. He certainly didn't like the thought that she might be out in the dark alone.

She wouldn't appreciate his concern. She'd tell

him he was being high-handed and a stick-in-the-mud and that her life was none of his business.

All of which was true. He placed his fingers on the key still stuck in the ignition of his car. He'd gone back and forth at least a hundred times since driving out here, telling himself he should go home and leave her to her own life.

Yes, he wanted to make sure she was okay. Despite her claim of experience, she seemed to have the self-preservation instinct of a lamb.

Maybe that was why he found her so fascinating. The women he'd known in his life who had been molded by difficult experiences were jaded and mistrustful. There was no edge to Tessa other than when she sparred with him. And that was like being poked by a toddler's rubber sword.

Lauren was at a sleepover again. Carson had offered to host the trio of little girls, but his daughter seemed horrified by the thought of her friends spending the night at their cabin.

"Sarah's mom makes s'mores and homemade crepes," Lauren had reported to him. As if that explained everything.

"I can make crepes," he said. "Or pancakes with faces made out of blueberries."

"You burn Pop-Tarts," his daughter reminded him.

"I did that once," he'd countered, "and I learned my lesson." He wanted to know his girl's friends but understood better than to push too hard. To be honest, he'd thought about asking Tessa for advice. There had been several times in the past week when Lauren had FaceTimed their neighbor to ask about homework or wardrobe choices or Tessa's opinion on a variety of topics.

He still wasn't sure about whether Tessa would end up a good influence, but so far he'd agreed with everything she'd told his daughter.

He'd turned on a baseball game earlier tonight and settled in with a beer and take-out Chinese from a restaurant in town. After the game, he hadn't been sleepy, more restless and on edge. He'd headed down the mountain, planning to pop into Trophy Room for a drink. At the last minute, he'd turned his car onto the highway that led east toward Montrose.

A couple came out of the bar followed by a group of rowdy young men. The man and woman held tight to each other while the friends laughed and pushed each other like a troop of bear cubs.

What were they laughing about? Had one of them asked Tessa for her number? Were these the kind of guys she would be interested in for the one-night stand she'd so brazenly advocated? Without giving himself too much time to think, Carson yanked the keys from the ignition and headed toward the front of the bar. It was nearly one thirty in the morning, and the place was still hopping.

He didn't immediately head to a stool but hung back until he saw Tessa carrying a tray of drinks to one of the four-tops near the dartboard. Carson made his way in that direction. He rubbed a hand over the back of his neck like he was just another customer with no specific agenda.

"Seriously?"

He turned at the sound of the familiar voice. Tessa's blue eyes blazed at him. He might be mistaken, but it felt like she was wearing slightly less makeup tonight. He didn't know why he liked that so much.

"Are you here to harass me again?"

"Harassment is a harsh accusation, Red."

"I'm well aware."

She smiled and waved a hand as two guys standing near the pool table called for another round.

"I'm busy, Carson. It's a half hour until last call and this is when things really pick up."

"I'll have a draft IPA," he told her. "Please. I assume you don't want to card me."

She rolled her eyes. "What I want is to stick the card… Never mind. One IPA coming up. Would you like some peanuts with that, sir?"

He shook his head. "No peanuts."

She brought him the beer after delivering a pitcher to the crowd at the pool table. Carson noticed she moved away quickly when one of the men made to reach for her. Had she learned the technique of dodging handsy guys at this job or from some other bar where she'd worked before now?

This was quite a bit different than he imagined her job as her sister's assistant.

"Thank you." He smiled when she handed him the beer then tried not to react as their fingers brushed and awareness rippled over his skin.

Tonight she wore another faded denim miniskirt and a tank top. It wasn't revealing but hugged her gentle curves in a way he found hard to resist. He shouldn't react so strongly. After all, he'd seen this woman naked coming out of the hot springs. At that point, it had been dark and he'd been so shocked at her boldness that his mind had gone blank.

Now his brain seemed intent on cataloging every tiny freckle that dotted her creamy skin.

"I hope they take care of you here. That you don't have to deal with guys hitting on you."

She tipped her chin. "I'm not going to have that argument with you again. This is my job and if you have a problem with it, go find another bar or drink at home. They sell peanuts in the grocery store, so there's very little you'd be missing."

"I'd be missing you," he said quietly. His blood ran hot when her lips parted on a soft inhalation.

"Let me know if you need anything else," she told him with a little less hostility. Then she turned and made the rounds of her section.

Carson sipped his beer and watched. She wasn't the most coordinated waitress he'd ever seen. She fumbled glasses and dropped crumpled up napkins on the ground. She also offered that bright smile to every one of her customers and her sweet presence seemed to make the dingy bar a little brighter.

Carson was fairly certain he wasn't the only one who noticed.

He caught quite a few men staring at her like lovesick puppies. She wasn't blatantly flirtatious but patted various arms and leaned in as customers talked, like she cared about what they were saying.

The Thirsty Chicken had a bouncer, a tan, bulky man with tattoos running the length of both arms. After watching for a while, Carson realized that the man did a pass of Tessa's section on a regular basis. He threw glares and subtle looks of warning at any customer who seemed to be getting too familiar with her.

There was an older waitress near the front of the bar but the bouncer didn't concern himself with her section. For some reason, it made Carson breathe a little easier that someone intimidating and potentially flat-out scary was looking after Tessa.

He stayed until last call. Not necessarily because it was part of his plan. He'd struck up a conversation with a couple of guys who worked as part of a local forest service crew. They talked about wildfire jobs in the area through the summer and the need for experienced pilots in the crew.

Carson didn't think that kind of work would suit his current lifestyle, but he was intrigued by it. Maybe if he found a way for a productive adrenaline rush, he wouldn't be so consumed with thoughts of his neighbor and the way she made his pulse race.

They also had suggestions for other routes he might pick up as far as transporting cargo. He took down a couple of names and contact information on his phone. As the bar lights flashed on and off signaling closing time, Carson's gaze immediately sought out Tessa. She was behind the bar straightening glasses.

He made his way slowly toward the front of the building.

"What branch?" the bouncer asked him as he was moving past.

"Navy," Carson answered automatically. "Is it that obvious?"

"An officer?"

"Lieutenant commander," Carson confirmed.

The bouncer nodded. "We don't get a lot of problems with officers. The young enlisted guys are occasionally another story, but I can handle it."

"You look like you could handle anything."

"You know Tessa?" The big guy scrubbed a hand

over his jaw. "I saw you talking to her and she kept glancing over at your table."

She'd been watching him the way he watched her? Good to know. Carson had been too busy trying not to get caught staring so he'd missed it.

"We're neighbors. She's friends with my daughter," he added, feeling like the bouncer was sizing him up. Trying to decide whether he was a threat to Tessa or not.

At that moment Carson didn't want to be a threat to her.

"I'm ready, Ron." Tessa flicked a dismissive glance at Carson. "Ron walks me to my car every night."

"I can do that," Carson offered.

Her shoulders went rigid. "That won't be—"

At that moment, a large crash sounded from the parking lot. Ron muttered a curse. "Nice to meet you, neighbor," he told Carson. "Stick close to our girl until she's safe in her car."

The bouncer trotted in the direction of the noise. Tessa blew out an exasperated breath then started toward the side of the building, not bothering to wait for Carson. He quickly caught up to her.

"You're very popular at the Thirsty Chicken."

If he were the withering sort, he would have collapsed under the sideline glare Tessa threw him. "Is that some sort of passive-aggressive way of criticizing me? Because I'm not going to apologize for being good at my job. I'm good at both of my jobs."

"No. I didn't mean it to come out that way." He shook his head. "Things often don't come out right around you. I just meant that it's clear people like you. Ron, the bouncer, was genuinely concerned for your well-being."

"He's a good guy."

"I agree," Carson said quietly. A moment later they made it to the Jeep.

Tessa unlocked the vehicle then turned to him. "What are you really doing here?"

"Lauren is at a sleepover. I wanted to get out of the house."

"Why not stay in Starlight? I'm sure you know plenty of people at Trophy Room."

"That's the problem," he admitted. "This is all new to me. Being a dad full-time and being part of a community, especially one as close-knit as Starlight. Sometimes it feels like I don't even fit into my own life. Other times I just want a break from the pressure of it." He massaged a hand over his jaw and looked out to the darkness beyond the parking lot, unable to meet her gaze. "That probably sounds stupid."

"It doesn't."

He glanced back at her. Was it his imagination or had she moved slightly closer? They stared at each other for several moments. The air grew thick with a connection he couldn't explain but was sick of fighting.

"Do you want to come over for a drink?" she asked suddenly.

Carson raised a brow.

"Just a drink," she clarified. "It takes me a while to wind down after I get off on busy nights. I usually watch reruns of lame sitcoms. If you want to watch TV with me, you can come over."

The light was dim in the parking lot, but he could still make out the way her cheeks flamed pink as she made the offer.

"I'd like that," he said, not allowing himself to worry about what he was getting himself into.

What in the heck had Tessa gotten herself into? She must have glanced in her rearview mirror one hundred times on the way back up the mountain. The headlights from Carson's truck were always shining, bold and steady in the darkness behind her.

She wasn't sure why she expected him to turn off. Maybe because he seemed smarter than her. She shouldn't rely on herself to make a smart decision. The whole reason she'd come to Starlight was to upend her life.

Carson seemed to be her total opposite, but now she almost wondered if that were true. She'd understood completely when he talked about not feeling comfortable in his own life. That understanding was what led her to invite him over.

Gosh, she hoped he didn't think she was extending an invitation for the random hookup she'd alluded to favoring. No. She'd made it clear. Television and a drink, although she wasn't sure what she had to offer him. Tessa rarely drank.

Hopefully, she'd have something left over from the last Chop It Like It's Hot meeting she'd hosted. Carson thought she was a bad girl. Women with experience probably didn't offer their guests a cup of chamomile tea late at night.

Butterflies flitted across her stomach as they passed his driveway. A tiny part of her thought he might bail at the last minute. She wouldn't care. It didn't matter to her if she watched TV with him or on her own.

Her body hummed with excitement even though she hated to admit it. She was only human after all, and Carson was undeniably handsome. She'd even seen him be charming, although never to her.

"What do you like?" he asked in that rumbly voice as they walked into the house.

Tessa wanted to fidget as an answering warmth spread low in her belly. Was he asking about what she liked in the bedroom or...?

Her mind went stubbornly blank. He gave her a knowing little smirk as if he knew exactly what she was thinking, which wasn't as disturbing as it probably should have been.

"Television shows," he clarified. "Personally, I'm a fan of *Seinfeld* but *How I Met Your Mother* is pretty good, too."

Tessa blinked. She couldn't believe they were talking about television shows. "*Friends*." Some of the tension balled inside her unfurled as she spoke the word. She could handle a normal conversation, but that might be about it, with her sexy neighbor.

He nodded. "I would have guessed that about you."

She placed her purse on the counter and flipped on the kitchen light. "Are you saying I'm predictable?"

Carson chuckled. "No, I would never say that about you, Red, but you have a Central Perk vibe."

"You know the name of the coffee shop?"

"Why does that surprise you?"

"Because you seem like the kind of guy who would only watch UFC fighting or hunting shows."

"That is definitely not a compliment."

"An observation," she admitted. "What can I get you to drink?" She held up a hand before he could answer. "Caveat, though. I'm not sure I have much to offer."

His brows drew together. "A beer?"

She opened the refrigerator. "How do you feel about cranberry juice?"

"That works, too."

"I'm normally well stocked," she lied, "but I'm running a little low on cash this month so..." She pulled the juice bottle from the refrigerator, wishing the cold air from the appliance would cool her nerves. She turned to Carson. "That's not true. I don't drink that much or often."

He inclined his head. "Okay."

"Does that surprise you?"

"Yes and no."

"What does that mean?"

"You talk a big talk, Red. So in that way, it surprises me. You talk about being a party girl. But the more I get to know you, nothing surprises me because I never know what to expect." He paused as if thinking about what he wanted to say next. "I guess you're pretty young to have given up drinking entirely if it was a part of your life. But kudos to you. I respect a person who can leave their demons behind."

Tessa's fingers fumbled on the glass she was pulling from the cabinet. Oh, her demons were riding shotgun every moment of her life. But there was no point in sharing that with Carson. She supposed it reflected well on her that he bought all of her lines. Although she knew at a deeper level, it didn't reflect well on her that she'd resorted to lying.

She thought about what both her sister and Madison had said. About staying in her own prison.

Maybe it was time to consider stepping out.

"I never drank. I never had a problem with it. I have kidney disease." She concentrated on pouring the juice as she said the words. "I received a transplant three years ago, but up until then, I spent most of my life sick. Drinking wasn't an option for me. I mean, everything's an option, but it wasn't good for my body."

She hazarded a glance and found that Carson's smoky gaze had gone almost black. She wasn't going to admit to anything more. For all he knew, she did the wild and crazy things he thought about her stone-cold sober.

"You're healthy now?"

She nodded around the emotion clogging her throat. "Yes." She was healthy. The fact that he focused on that fact first meant something to her. Most people immediately went to sympathy or wanting to know how hard her life had been and how she dealt with it.

"Do you want to talk about it?"

She breathed out a laugh. "Not at the moment." What she wanted was to rush around the counter and throw herself into Carson's arms. She'd never felt this sort of desire deep within her. Not for a man, anyway. She'd yearned to be normal. Although she'd had crushes on boys in high school and college, nobody had ever affected her the way her neighbor did.

He picked up the juice glass from the counter. "Let me know if you do. I'm not the greatest listener in the world, but the dad thing is helping me not be so horrible at it."

"You're trying," she told him gently. "That counts for a lot."

It was more than her parents had done. They loved her, but they'd never tried to understand her or show any respect for her wishes about her life.

"*Big Bang Theory*," Carson said into the silence that had fallen between them.

Tessa felt a grin spread across her face. "*Big Bang Theory* it is," she said and led the way to her cozy family room area.

They settled on opposite sides of the couch as Tessa's girl parts screamed in silent protest. Get closer to that gorgeous man, they commanded.

She flipped on the television and ignored her hormones, surprised to find that easier said than done. Then the show started, Sheldon cracked the first joke, and Tessa realized that even with her pent-up frustration, there was no place she'd rather be or anyone she could imagine wanting to be with more.

Chapter Nine

As the credits rolled on the final episode of season three, arguably the best of the series, Tessa yawned then covered her mouth, hoping Carson didn't notice. "Do we start on season four?" she asked.

He breathed out a small laugh and picked up the remote from where it sat on the couch between them. "You've yawned twenty-five times in the past twenty-two minutes," he reported.

"You were counting?"

"Rough estimate. I think you've wound down from earlier."

She had. In fact, she was having trouble keeping her eyes open. But she didn't want this night to end. She liked having the company. As much as she appreciated living on her own after two decades in her parents' house, she missed the companionship.

A couple of months ago, Cory had moved in with her for a short time while she and Jordan were working things out. That's when Tessa had discovered she wasn't quite as much of a lone wolf as she liked to fancy herself.

Once her body had resigned itself to a platonic evening on the couch with Carson, she'd enjoyed having him there. He laughed at the right times and made funny comments about some of her favorite episodes.

She really would have pegged him for a sports-only kind of guy. He needed to stop having these onion-like layers, because they just made her want to peel them back.

He stood then offered her his hand. "Thanks for the juice," he said as he pulled her to her feet.

"You're welcome." They stood toe-to-toe, and her body instantly reawakened. It congratulated her for not totally messing up its chance for a little some-thing-something with the hottie neighbor.

"It's nothing."

Carson frowned. "What's nothing?"

Oh, Lord, she had said that out loud. She gave him a bright smile and backed away. "The glass of juice. It's nothing to share a glass of juice. Just being neighborly." In her sleepy state and haste to get away, her heel caught on the corner of the coffee table leg and she stumbled. Why did Carson have this kind of an effect on her?

He steadied her easily, but the assistance ended with her plastered against the front of him. To her surprise, he didn't immediately release her. His arm tightened around her waist like he didn't want to let her go.

"Your coordination leaves something to be desired," he told her, his voice barely above a whisper.

"Maybe I did it on purpose so we'd end up like this."

"Devious," he murmured. "Good to know."

She almost laughed at the absurdity of that, but all thoughts of humor faded with the way he was looking at her. "Yeah," she agreed. "I'm devious."

She expected him to call her out on the obvious lie. By now he had to know her well enough to understand that wasn't true. Instead, he leaned in until his mouth was a whisper away from hers. The spicy male scent of him enveloped her, and his warm breath on her face made goose bumps erupt along her skin.

"I like it," he told her then pressed his mouth to hers.

Tessa might be inexperienced, but she'd at least been kissed. Although never like this. Carson didn't shove his tongue down her throat or taste like corn chips. She got the barest hint of the tang of juice mixed with minty gum. Some cologne manufacturer needed to hear about the combination because it was a heck of an appealing turn-on. His full lips were soft and searching like he wanted to memorize the feel of her lips against his. He nipped at the corner of her mouth and she let out a soft groan.

The heat swirling through her body was like nothing she'd ever experienced.

No wonder all of the girls in her high school had spent so much time in the locker room before and after gym class rating the boys who kissed well in their class. Tessa imagined that Carson would have been at the top of the list.

He lifted a hand and smoothed his fingers over her cheek. "Relax," he urged. "This doesn't have to mean you like me."

She did like him. Far too much.

She also tried her best to quiet her mind. It wasn't easy. She was so used to leading with her brain. Now that she was ready to give full control to her body she realized she didn't quite know how that worked.

So she focused on Carson and on the way his mouth felt against hers. How could a man who was all hard planes and edges have such a soft mouth? She ran her tongue along the seam of it because she couldn't help herself. He seemed to take that as an invitation, which she was eternally grateful for because heat warmed her belly as he deepened the kiss.

He drew her even closer, and she felt the evidence of his arousal pressing against her belly. This time when her mind tried to send up warning flags, her body knocked each one of them down like a skier racing through a giant slalom course. She was barreling down a mountain of desire and didn't even care that she had no idea whether she was heading for a photo finish or the side of a cliff.

He shifted and then lowered himself to the sofa, taking Tessa with him. She straddled his legs and ran her hands through his thick hair as they kissed. His palm grazed the sensitive tip of one nipple through the thin cotton of the tank top she wore. It was another layer of sensation swirling through her, and she breathed out his name on a needy puff of air.

There was a low growl in response. It gave her a feeling of heady power to know he was as caught up in this moment as her. They stayed that way, discovering each other, for minutes or maybe hours. She'd never truly given herself over to physical sensation and reveled in the moment. Carson's hand moved under her shirt and up her rib cage. She loved the feel of the weight of her breasts in his big hands. She wanted more. At that moment she wanted everything.

Her denim skirt had hitched around her hips, and when he trailed a finger toward the apex of her thighs, she tipped up her hips to give him better access. It was as if her body knew what to do even if her rational brain wasn't quite sure. Tessa was beginning to understand that in certain situations brain cells were overrated.

She knew he'd be able to tell how aroused she was. The idea of it should have embarrassed her, but he let out a little groan of satisfaction as his fingers pushed aside her panties while he kissed her even more deeply. She sucked in a ragged breath as he traced circles around her most private area.

"So damn beautiful," he whispered. Tessa couldn't even take time to revel in the compliment. She was too busy losing her mind and her control with the way he touched her. She began to move in a steady rhythm and when Carson's fingers brushed her center, it was only a moment until a soul-shattering release coursed through her.

Tessa cried out his name and he held her even more tightly if that were possible. It took her a minute to come back down to earth. Finally, she did and realized he'd stilled below her. Simply holding her, pressing tiny kisses to her forehead and cheeks.

"I'm sorry," she said automatically, scrambling to move off him. At first, he held on but when she pulled away again, he released her to sit next to him on the couch.

"What in the world would you be apologizing

for after that?" He sounded genuinely baffled and scrubbed a hand over his face like he was trying to pull himself back together.

"I didn't mean to…it was fast…you didn't even…" She darted a glance at his lap, and clearly he was still aroused. "I owe you something or we can…"

"Tessa, stop. I'm plenty satisfied with this night. More than you could know if I had to guess. There's no rush for anything else."

For her there was. A big part of her wanted to rush through the actual act so she could just call it good and have the whole V-card thing a part of her past.

Carson adjusted himself, then shifted so that he was facing her.

"You don't owe me anything, Red. Let's get that straight, and for the record, you don't owe any man ever. If a guy makes you feel like you do, run the other direction."

Embarrassment crackled through her, hot and sparking like electricity. Of course she knew she didn't owe him. But she wanted something from him that she couldn't quite articulate. Mostly she wanted more of the confidence she'd felt when she was losing herself in his arms and because of his touch.

For those minutes, Tessa wasn't faking anything. She wasn't pretending to be somebody new or reaching for a version of herself she wasn't sure she could even live up to. It had all been real and authentic, and she'd liked herself at that moment. She liked herself with him.

"I know that." She got up from the couch and adjusted her skirt and top. Her legs felt heavy but irritation propelled her forward. "So I guess this is the point where I say now that I've gotten what I wanted, you can hit the road. And don't let the door—"

"I get the message." Carson stood as well, but he didn't look put out by her rude reaction. If anything, he seemed more amused, like she was a silly puppy nipping at his heels.

She felt absurd and prickly and not nearly as satisfied as she had minutes earlier. Something was missing, and she hated that she didn't know enough to even understand what it was.

"I had fun tonight," he told her as he moved past.

"It doesn't mean anything," she felt compelled to say. Another lie.

"Whatever you want to believe," he agreed then headed out the door. "See you around, Red."

As soon as she was alone, Tessa ran for the bathroom.

She flipped on the light and examined herself in the mirror that hung above the vessel sink. Did she look different? More worldly? She'd never gone that far with a guy and what she knew of her body was from furtive touches in the dark of her bedroom.

Of course it had meant something. At the very

least it meant a man might want to kiss her. Might be attracted to her. She sucked in a hollow breath and reached for the waistband of her skirt. She undid the button, unzipped it and pushed it down her hips. She lifted her shirt to gaze at the scars on her stomach. Of course they were always there. She'd had her first surgery at age seven and nearly a dozen more after that.

But she'd stopped looking at her body. She didn't need a visible reminder of what she'd been through. Now that she had gone that far with Carson, she wondered what would happen if he had stayed and there'd been more. She couldn't possibly let him see her body, could she? She didn't want to remind him or anyone of the part of her life that defined her.

She ran a finger along the most recent scar. The one from the kidney transplant surgery. It was faded to a silvery color now, and she wondered what the corresponding scar on her father's abdomen looked like.

She pressed on it and sighed. It didn't hurt any longer. But what would Carson think? What would any man think of her battered body?

Automatically, she reached out and flipped off the bathroom light. The room plunged into darkness, and Tessa nodded. That was the answer. She would have sex in the dark. Only ever in the dark. She pulled up her skirt and exited the bathroom without bothering to turn on the light again.

And whether he knew it or not, Carson was going to be the man she was with in that way for her first time. He proved tonight that he knew his way around a woman's body although she still wasn't even sure if he liked her. That's why he was the perfect candidate. A man who would be good in bed but not expect anything more. Now she just needed to go about seducing him.

Carson was a failure as a father.

He glanced toward the side of the soccer field where Lauren stood comforting one of the other girls on her new team. He cringed as his daughter shot him a death glare that would have melted the skin off a lesser man.

A heavy hand landed on his shoulder, and he turned to see Josh Johnson, another volunteer youth soccer coach, offering him a sympathetic smile.

"How do you feel about being the snack parent?" Josh asked, giving a mock shudder. "Because I think your coaching days are over."

Carson nodded. "I didn't mean to make her cry."

"Buddy, you made half the team cry."

"They were doing cartwheels on the field," Carson said, as if that was a defense. "I was just trying to get their attention."

"They're on a beginner rec league team," Josh reminded him. "Cartwheels and daisy picking are part of the deal."

"What about winning?"

The other man chuckled. "You've got a lot to learn."

Josh had no idea how true that statement was. Sadly, Carson had been proud of himself going into practice. He'd signed Lauren up for a late-spring soccer league and when the woman taking her registration had mentioned the team where his daughter would be slotted didn't have a coach, Carson had immediately volunteered. He'd played soccer in high school and messed around on a couple of club teams during his time in the navy.

How hard could it be to teach the basics to a group of elementary school kids?

Harder than learning to fly an F-16 he discovered very quickly. Josh, who was coaching his own daughter's team on the other side of the community park, had taken pity on him and come over to offer some tips.

Carson had met the other single dad in town and appreciated his friendly nature but wasn't looking to necessarily be a part of some sort of single dad posse. He'd made excuses when Josh had invited him out for a beer along with his brother and a local attorney and a couple of other guys in town.

Carson wished he had a beer right now or maybe a sledgehammer to knock himself out.

"Looks like your cavalry has arrived," Josh said, an odd note of tension in his voice.

Carson looked over to the sidelines again to see Tessa and her friend Ella talking to the girls. The team had gathered around the two women and Lauren smiled as Tessa hugged her and then said something that made all the girls laugh.

Based on the looks a couple of the players lobbed in his direction, he had to guess he was the butt of whatever joke had just been told. Fine. He'd take it. Anything so that the girls wouldn't be crying when their parents arrived to pick them up.

Tessa and Ella led the girls back out onto the field. Tessa gave a few instructions and the girls started on a passing drill. Ella walked toward Carson and Josh, leaving Tessa on her own with the team.

Carson wasn't sure parents were going to approve of that any more than the crying he realized as he looked more closely at her not that it was anyone's business. She wore actual leather leggings with a herringbone pattern and tank top that showed little glimpses of the red bra she had on underneath.

At least she was wearing sneakers. Her outfit seemed as though it would be more appropriate paired with stiletto heels or something equally as appealing.

"It sounds like you're making a play for coach of the year," Ella said to Carson when she was a few feet away.

"He's doing fine," Josh answered before Carson had a chance. "He just needs a little more training."

"That's your specialty, I assume."

Carson looked back and forth between the two of them. He knew Ella was a tough cookie based on the small amount of time he'd spent with her, but Josh gave the immediate impression of being a giant teddy bear. Not so much teddy and a lot more angry bear as he looked at Ella.

"I've got it covered." Josh said the words with more confidence than Carson felt. Certainly more confidence than Josh had shown before Ella arrived at the scene.

"I think you owe Tessa a big thank-you." Ella spoke directly to Carson, ignoring Josh. "She's got a way with kids."

She had a way with everyone as far as Carson could tell.

Josh made a snide comment about Ella's outfit, and she immediately went off on a long diatribe about how badly he needed a haircut.

Carson decided he'd leave the two of them to whatever they had going on and jogged toward Tessa. The team immediately stopped moving.

"It's okay," Tessa called. "Keep going. They look great, right, Coach?"

"Great," he shouted, trying to sound upbeat. The girl closest to him flinched. "Great," he repeated in a softer tone.

Tessa's summer-sky gaze danced as he moved closer. "Finally, I've discovered something you suck at."

The comment shocked a laugh out of him. "I didn't know you were looking for my flaws. I have many, by the way."

She made a noncommittal sound, which made his heart stutter. He was far from perfect, but he liked the idea of her thinking about his positive traits. He liked it more than he should.

"Thanks for bailing me out," he said then looked over his shoulder to where Josh and Ella stood, clearly engaged in a heated conversation. "Apparently, I'm going to be relegated to providing snacks."

"Make sure they're organic," Tessa advised after calling out encouragement to one of the girls as she tripped then recovered her balance. "That's a big deal to parents."

"Organic," he repeated, committing it to memory. "Did you play soccer?" he asked after she gave a few coaching instructions to the team. The girls started on another drill.

"You're joking, right? Remember that I didn't

know getting the ball down field was called dribbling. Or maybe I knew and had blocked it out."

"You seem to know a lot about the game right now."

"My sister played. I watched from the sidelines. I wasn't allowed to do any activity where I potentially could have been knocked in the stomach."

Right. He'd forgotten what she'd shared about having kidney disease. Not exactly forgotten but thoughts of her coming apart in his arms had seemed to burn away any other details from their time together Friday night.

"Well, you obviously picked up a lot from being a fan." He noticed that a group of parents had gathered near the parking lot and glanced at his watch. "Practice time is over," he said on a sigh. "Thank God."

"I'm going to gather the girls so you can apologize," Tessa told him.

"I didn't mean to make them cry." He repeated the words he'd said to Josh.

"I know. Now make it better."

Before he could protest, she lifted two fingers to her mouth and let out an impressive whistle. The girls gathered in a circle around Tessa, like tiny moths to their soccer guru flame. Carson eased back, hoping she'd just finish things up. Instead she reached out and pulled him closer.

He mustered his courage and looked each girl

in the eyes as he offered a sincere apology. Most of them nodded and one of the smaller ones gave him a tentative hug. Then they headed toward the parking lot as if all was forgiven.

"Good job, Daddy," Lauren told him. "But don't make the team cry again, okay?"

"Okay, sweetheart."

She nodded. "I'm going to collect the rest of the cones."

Tessa gave him a teasing elbow to the ribs. "Nice work, Coach. I'm proud of you."

He gazed down at her, wondering if she knew how much those words meant to him. Without even trying, Tessa had become important in his life, and he wasn't sure what to do next.

Chapter Ten

"We brought you cookies."

"What happened to your face?"

Tessa lifted her fingers to her cheek then grimaced as she remembered the face mask she'd slathered on her skin a few minutes earlier.

Seriously, Carson Campbell was a problem for her. She lost all cognitive function when he was around.

She focused her attention on Lauren, instead, as she flipped shut her laptop.

She'd been sitting on one of the rocking chairs on the cabin's front porch, bundled up in a thick sweater, leggings and fuzzy boots, working out a few travel details for her sister's upcoming book tour.

"I love cookies," she told the girl.

"Me, too." Lauren smiled like it was some kind of special bond they shared.

Carson continued to study her. "Your face is blue."

She hadn't seen him since the soccer practice, and that was by her own choice.

He'd actually knocked on her door the next morning, but she hadn't answered. After last Friday night, she was still trying to figure out how to best go about getting him to agree to sleep with her. Maybe it wouldn't be that hard.

He was a guy, and things were pretty straightforward from their end. But as much as it seemed like a perfect way to check one of the biggest to-dos off her bucket list, when it came down to it, she felt nervous. And when Tessa was nervous, she talked too much. Until she figured out how she was going to handle things, she decided it would be better to avoid him.

"They're chocolate chip," Lauren said, climbing the porch steps. "We had to bake more because Dad put salt instead of sugar in the first batch."

"They looked the same to me," Carson said, throwing up his hands.

Despite not wanting to feel any connection to him, Tessa was charmed by the way the tips of his ears turned pink with embarrassment. "I guess it's just another thing I'm not good at," he said, giving her an arch look.

"Can I do a face mask?" Lauren asked.

"We're just here to deliver the cookies," Carson told his daughter. "I'm sure Tessa has lots going on."

"Are you getting ready for a date?" Lauren's abrupt question shocked Tessa as well as Carson based on the look he gave her.

She rose from the swing. "No date. Not with my face covered in blue stuff."

"Mommy always does more beauty stuff before a date," Lauren explained. "So she didn't look old or like she had a kid."

Tessa's heart ached at the way the girl said it so matter-of-factly. Lauren's mother had taken steps to identify herself as someone who wasn't a mom and had no problem letting her daughter know it. Tessa could not understand that sort of thinking.

"Do you want to come in and have a cookie and a glass of milk?"

Lauren was hard to resist, the sweet child clearly missing her mother even though Carson's ex seemed like a real piece of work as far as Tessa was concerned.

"Maybe we can convince your dad to try a face mask."

Carson chuckled and shook his head. "I don't think so."

"Yeah." Lauren grabbed her father's hand. "Let's do one together, Daddy."

Carson looked like he wanted to argue, but Tessa knew he wouldn't. The guy was a total pushover when it came to his girl.

"Cookies and milk and a face mask. This is what my life has come to."

"I have beer," Tessa told him as they walked into the house. "I can offer you cookies and beer."

Carson made a show of glancing at his watch. "Look at that. It's five-o-four. I guess a beer would be fun."

Tessa started to smile but then remembered the mask as her face crinkled. "My time is up with this mask. Carson, the milk and the beer are both in the fridge. Help yourselves. I'll get this washed off and then I'll bring the supplies out and we can have our father-daughter mini spa night."

"Awesome," Lauren said.

"Mini spa night," Carson repeated. "Not the sort of activity I ever expected to join in on."

"There's a first time for everything."

He gave her a funny look and Tessa rushed out of the kitchen. There was no way he could know about her inexperience. At least she didn't think that would be possible.

But the words reminded her of what she wanted from him, which had the flock of nerves taking wing across her stomach once again. She used a washcloth to wipe the mask off her face then dabbed some moisturizer on her skin. She was planning to add a little lip gloss and mascara because she'd gotten used to wearing some type of makeup, but Lauren appeared at the bathroom door.

"I brought you a cookie," the girl said as she munched on the piece in her mouth. "You were taking too long."

"Um, thanks."

Tessa swallowed hard as Carson appeared behind his daughter in the narrow hall. He tipped the can of beer to his mouth, and she watched with fascination from the reflection in the mirror as his Adam's apple bobbed. What an inopportune time to have the urge to kiss him there.

Or at all.

She forced her attention back to Lauren. "Do you want hydration or brightening?"

The girl's eyes widened. "I don't know."

"Well, your skin is perfect to start with so let's use different criteria for choosing. Blue or pink?"

"Blue."

"Nice." Tessa pulled two jars from the drawer in the bathroom vanity. "That leaves pink for your dad."

"No, thanks." Carson shook his head. "I think I'll just watch."

"You have to try it," Lauren urged. "Come on, Daddy. Please."

Tessa bit down on her lip to keep from smiling. How could he resist that kind of a plea?

"Fine, but this stays between the three of us."

Carson rubbed a hand across his jaw later that night as he stood in his kitchen watching Tessa and Lauren at the table, their heads bent close together. As if she could feel the weight of his gaze, Tessa glanced up and smiled. "You feel soft like a baby's butt, right?"

He chuckled at the disturbing image. "Not exactly, but I feel soft."

"I feel like a baby's butt," Lauren said proudly.

He still wasn't sure how he felt about his daughter's obvious adoration for their spunky neighbor. But he couldn't deny things were easier when Lauren was in a good mood, and Tessa helped with that immensely.

They'd put on face masks, and Tessa had painted Lauren's fingernails while Carson fixed the squeaky fan in her bathroom. He was glad to repay her in some way for entertaining his kid, not to mention him. Both Lauren and Tessa had found it infinitely amusing to see his face covered with pink goop. Even now, he caught the faint scent of the fruit-punch face mask she'd used on him after insisting that he start with a blueberry facial scrub.

He'd almost been tempted to take a selfie and send

it to a few of his military buddies. They would have gotten a kick out of him in that kind of shape. But the moment had somehow been too sweet for that. There simply weren't enough times when he saw his daughter truly relaxed, and he didn't want to taint that with any distractions.

After they'd finished with the spa activities, Lauren had invited Tessa to dinner at their house. She'd tried to decline, but his daughter was persistent when she made up her mind.

One of the wives of a pilot he worked with had given him a whole bunch of casseroles that could be frozen to eat later. He knew it didn't say much about his domestic skills that a woman he'd never even met had taken pity on him, but she was a fantastic cook. Tonight they'd dined on smothered enchiladas. He'd at least had the forethought to buy a bag of salad and some chips to round out the meal.

Lauren had quickly finished her homework while Tessa and Carson cleaned up after dinner. She wanted to show Tessa some new dance channel on YouTube and Carson made a mental note to recheck the parental controls he had on the internet at the cabin.

The two ladies stood and propped up the device against a napkin holder at the center of the table while they tried to follow along with the dance they were learning.

"You should try this with us," Tessa said. The color was high on her cheeks. "It's kind of unfair that you're watching while we embarrass ourselves."

"Dad doesn't dance," Lauren said and there was that switch from daddy to dad again like some sort of subtle reminder of her tacit disapproval.

"For your information, I'm an excellent dancer. I can macarena with the best of them."

Lauren's brow furrowed. "What are you even talking about?"

Tessa's smile widened, and she gestured to him. "But have you done *the savage*?" she asked.

"No," he answered even as he moved forward. She was becoming as irresistible to him as his daughter when she crooked a finger in that way. When the hell had he become such a softy?

He stood behind the two of them and did his best to follow along with the trendy millennials on the small screen. It felt like just a bunch of silly hand movements and hip thrusts. He didn't think his ten-year-old daughter should be hip thrusting, but she was laughing hysterically, the sound so beautiful to him that he couldn't complain. They continued dancing until all of them were sweaty and out of breath. Carson was laughing so hard his side hurt. He hadn't laughed like that in ages.

As Lauren closed out of the app, Tessa's gaze met his and darkened in a way he quite enjoyed. She straightened one of the chairs at the table and made a show of glancing at her watch.

"I should go," she said. "I'm meeting some friends at Trophy Room tonight."

"The playoff game," he said. "You've already missed the first half."

"Exactly. That's why I need to go." She hugged Lauren. "Thank you so much for inviting me to dinner. And for the cookies. It was an honor to help out with your soccer team. I'm sure you guys will have a great season."

Lauren sent Carson a sidelong glance. "We kind of need a new coach."

His good mood dimmed ever so slightly at the reminder of how he'd messed that up.

"Your dad will figure it out." Tessa sounded so sure.

He wished he could have that sort of confidence in himself. "Head upstairs and brush your teeth," he told his daughter. "I'll be up in a few minutes."

Lauren grabbed her iPad.

"Devices stay in the kitchen overnight," he reminded her.

She rolled her eyes but didn't argue. A moment later, he and Tessa were alone in the kitchen.

"I've really got to go," she said.

"Should be a big crowd in town tonight." He followed her toward the front of the cabin.

"I guess."

"It will probably beat hanging out with me on your couch in the fun category." He could have smacked himself on the head as soon as the words were out of his mouth. Was he fishing for a compliment or just wanting to remind her of what had happened between them before she headed out to a bar where she might meet another guy?

"I doubt that," she said quietly, "but it will be safer for my sanity."

And on those parting words, she walked out the door.

"That hottie at the bar is checking you out," Ella told Tessa an hour later. They were seated at a booth with Ella's sister-in-law, Kaitlyn, and her friend Mara, who was married to local attorney Parker Johnson, Josh's brother.

"Beefy lumberjacks aren't my type," Tessa said as she glanced toward the bar. Indeed, the man with the thick beard and a flannel shirt covering his broad shoulders made eye contact with her and tipped his beer bottle in her direction.

She flashed a perfunctory smile and looked away. What in the world was the matter with her? Hot lumberjacks should be her type. Any single available man should be her type. One of her main goals for a fresh start in life had been to figure out her place in the dating world. She'd even considered trying her hand at a singles app when she'd first come to Starlight, but she'd never quite gotten around to creating a profile.

Now she couldn't muster a bit of interest even though her friends stared at her like she'd lost her mind. Maybe she had. She'd lost it for her strong and steady neighbor. A man who wanted a woman in his life completely different from the kind of woman Tessa was determined to be.

"An interesting turn of events," Ella murmured before taking a sip of her margarita.

"Speaking of hot men," Mara said as she popped a peanut into her mouth, "pickup from soccer practice was all atwitter the other night discussing the new volunteer coach and his too-pretty-for-their-own-good new assistants."

Ella groaned. "Do not tell me that the mom brigade noticed us at soccer practice. I want to be on the mom radar in this town like I want to stick a fork in my eye."

"Oh, you're on it," Mara said with a laugh.

Ella pointed at Tessa. "I am never helping you out with your neighbor and his cute kid again."

"What's so bad about the mom brigade?" Tessa asked. "I get it if you're a single guy in there like the sharks swimming with fresh meat in the water. But you're probably harmless to other women."

"Not according to a few of the moms in Starlight," Mara explained. "It's a great small town but some of the social circles can be tough to crack. Trust me, I've been there and done that." She took a small sip of her drink. "Single dads are different. Josh said the parents voted to keep Carson as the coach even though he made the girls cry."

Tessa cringed. "He apologized. He didn't mean it."

Mara shrugged. "I'm not sure it would have mattered if he did. There are two single moms in his daughter's age group and if they've decided they like him then there's not much anyone else can do about it."

A hot flash of jealousy roared through Tessa. "It's not right to objectify people."

"I agree." Mara pushed the basket of peanuts to the other side of the table. "I need these taken away so I'm not tempted. I've heard plenty of stories from Josh about the lengths women have gone to get his attention. And he's just an average-looking guy. I've seen that Carson Campbell. He's a hunk and a half."

Ella snorted. "Don't use the word *hunk* because it sounds like something your grandmother would say, and Josh isn't average looking. I'm sure lots of women find him very attractive."

Mara's mouth curved at one side but she quickly flattened it again. "I'm sure."

"No more talk about hot men." Tessa inclined her

head toward the bar. "Even the lumberjack variety. I want to enjoy time with my friends and the game. I love hockey."

"It's the basketball playoffs tonight." Mara pointed to one of the flat-screen TVs hung around the bar. Clearly, Tessa hadn't been paying attention. "Game four."

"Right," Tessa agreed and lifted her Shirley Temple high. "A toast to game four."

Chapter Eleven

"Come on, Dad. I have to get faster."

Carson lined up the cones in the driveway the way Lauren commanded even as he shook his head. "Sweetheart, you are doing great in practice. You even scored a goal."

"Only because Chloe was distracted by a butterfly that landed on the goalpost. She was protecting it and not the goal."

Carson had noticed that but didn't acknowledge it right now. What would be the point of that?

"Some of the girls already don't like me because you made them cry. I need to be good so I can stay on the team."

Just what he needed—another reminder of how he'd messed up so badly at her first soccer practice. Josh had helped him with the next one. Oddly, Carson didn't want to give up his role, and was going to do his best to emulate Josh's calm demeanor with the girls. It was a stretch, but he wouldn't give up.

"It's a little too early to set up a drivers ed parallel parking course."

He and Lauren both turned at the sound of Tessa's voice. She was coming up the hill in running shorts and an athletic tank top. Her hair was pulled back into a braid, and by the look of glistening sweat on her skin and the rosy glow on her face, it was clear she'd been out for a jog.

"It's so I can train and get faster," Lauren said proudly. "I'm gonna be a real athlete just like you."

Tessa's expression softened at his daughter's words. There was no denying how much it meant to him that Tessa was so sweet with Lauren. He might not be certain that she was the best influence, but he appreciated her kindness toward his girl.

"I was never much of an athlete," Tessa said as she got closer. She put her hands on her hips and rolled her shoulders. "Just know it's never too late. Lauren, you can do whatever you set your mind to."

Carson wanted to believe that was true but he had no facts to back it up, not when he understood the asthma that plagued his daughter could rear its ugly head at any time.

In her workout gear with her long legs and lean muscles, Tessa looked like an athlete. She didn't look like somebody who had spent most of her life sick. He once again admired her resolve in making her life into what she wanted it to be.

Tessa patted Lauren's shoulder. "I think your dedication is amazing. Maybe you'd like a training buddy?"

Lauren's face lit with excitement at the offer. It was clear by the way Tessa glanced in his direction with a sheepish grimace that she'd made it without considering his potential disapproval.

I'm sorry, she mouthed before turning to Lauren again. "Actually, you and your dad can probably handle it. He can run you through some of his navy exercises."

He laughed. "Let's work up to that."

"Daddy, can Tessa work out with me? Please."

He should probably be offended that his kid was more interested in spending time with their neighbor than her own father, but even he couldn't deny that Tessa made everything more fun.

"I'll put you both through your paces," he told Lauren with a wink.

Tessa gamely helped set up the makeshift speed

and agility course then followed Lauren through it with a smile on her face.

They were on their third lap around the course when the wheezing started. Lauren stopped running and clutched at her chest. The struggle to draw in a full breath was almost tangible and he and Tessa both rushed to her side.

"The inhaler is in the top drawer in the upstairs bathroom," Carson told Tessa. "I forgot to have her take a couple puffs before we came out."

He knew this was a risk and cursed himself for not remembering the inhaler earlier, at the same time wondering if Lauren had been completely honest about her mother's reasons for not letting her take part in organized sports.

Disliking weekend game times was one thing, but watching his little girl struggle for each breath terrified him to his core. It was a fear he couldn't seem to control although the rational part of his brain knew the inhaler should give her relief.

Tessa returned a minute later and he handed the device to Lauren, who did her best to breathe in the puffs of medicine as she sat in the grass. To Carson's horror, her breathing didn't calm right away. She dispensed another pump, and finally, the wheezing disappeared and she breathed more deeply.

"I'm fine," she said after a moment.

She didn't look fine. His precious baby looked

like death warmed over. He pressed his open palm to her cheek, which was clammy now.

"You are a brave kid," Tessa said when the silence stretched so long it felt awkward.

"I don't like that feeling," Lauren said, pushing her hair away from her face. "What if it happens when I'm playing soccer? I can't score if I can't breathe."

"You shouldn't play," Carson said without hesitation. "Your mom told me that your asthma attacks are often triggered by physical exercise. I should have thought about that. You should never have been put in the position I put you in tonight, sweetheart. I'll call the rec center tomorrow and—"

"I want to play." Lauren clenched her fingers around her inhaler as she gave him a mulish glare. "You can't say no. No take-backs."

"Your health isn't worth it. You just said you're worried about not being able to breathe on the soccer field."

"I'm worried about not being able to score," Lauren countered. "That's not the same thing. I want to play."

"No."

"Daddy, you can't say no."

The panic squeezing his heart made him careless with his words. "I just did. Easily. I'll say it again. No."

Lauren turned and kicked one of the cones, threw her inhaler into the yard and ran for the house.

"Don't run," he shouted after her. "Be careful of your breathing."

That command made her run faster, the door slamming behind her with a harsh smack that reverberated in the quiet she'd left behind.

"Damn it," he muttered, wanting to kick his own stupid cone.

He could feel the weight of Tessa's gaze and forced himself to look at her. "She can't play," he said through clenched teeth.

"Are you certain?"

"You saw her. She could barely breathe. Am I supposed to let that happen on the regular?"

"Have you seen an allergist since you've been in Starlight?"

He shook his head.

Tessa righted the cone Lauren had knocked over. Her tone was almost achingly gentle when she spoke. "Maybe you should start there before you forbid her from being a normal kid."

"She's normal."

"She won't feel normal if you put limits on her," Tessa countered. "Trust me, I know. I also know people with asthma—even when it's serious—lead normal, active lives. It would be in your daughter's best interest, as well as yours, to work with her on finding a solution instead of against her."

"I'm not against her. I'm for her being able to breathe. She can't breathe if she has asthma attacks every time she runs."

"Is it every time?" Tessa inclined her head. "She ran in practice the other night, right?"

He gave a reluctant nod.

"Are there other options as far as positions she could play on the team? Goalie or defense? Something where she wouldn't be running up and down the entire field?"

"I suppose." Carson massaged a hand over the back of his neck. Some of the panic he'd felt minutes ago subsided, lulled by Tessa's calm and rational take on the situation. It felt as though he had no ability to be rational when it came to Lauren.

She stepped closer to him and gave him a tight hug. The amount of comfort he took from her embrace shocked him. He wasn't a hugger by nature. But it was a huge relief to not feel so alone in dealing with this moment.

"Do you really think she can play sports and stay healthy?"

She drew away and nodded. "I think it's worth investigating Lauren's options. It's important to her."

"Can't I just make some more damn felt animals?

Hell, I'll learn to knit a scarf if it would make her happy."

"She wants to play soccer. Somehow I don't think she's going to be swayed."

He glanced at the house. "She gets that stubborn streak from her mother."

Tessa grinned at him. "Yeah, right."

"She hates me again," he said with a sigh.

"Go find her and start the research together. Do a search on playing soccer with asthma and see what you find. What she wants is to know you believe in her. She wants you to help her have the life she wants, not to keep her limited by her illness."

"Like what happened to you."

She shrugged and looked away like she didn't want him to see what her gaze would reveal. "Let's just say I feel confident giving advice in this circumstance."

Carson wasn't used to taking advice. Soldiering through without anyone's help was more his style. But all the rules had changed when Lauren came to live with him. And as much as he didn't want to admit it, Tessa was changing them again.

He liked to believe he was a man of reasonable intelligence. At least he knew enough to try with his daughter.

"If I can help in any way, I will," Tessa offered almost shyly. "I know I'm not who you want—"

"Thank you." He punctuated those two words with a quick kiss pressed to her lush mouth. "Somehow you're always coming to my rescue."

She grinned at that then schooled her features like her smile had revealed too much. Apparently he wasn't the only one trying to fight the connection that seemed to grow stronger every time they were together. "Just being neighborly," she told him then took a step back. "I should go. Big plans tonight."

"Oh, yeah?"

"A hot date."

"Oh."

His mood deflated like a day-old balloon. He shouldn't care about her plans. They were none of his business. His heart couldn't seem to grasp that message. "Thanks again for the advice, Tessa. Have a good time on your date."

He didn't like the thought of her potentially in another man's arms after what they'd shared but had no right to complain. "Don't get too wild and crazy," he said as he began to collect the cones, proud that he kept his tone light, even teasing, like he might have been talking to a little sister instead of the woman who had him tied in knots.

"Sure," she agreed with a similar amount of forced cheer. "Good luck with Lauren."

He nodded and watched her jog to the end of his driveway and turn up the hill toward her house. He wanted to call after her and tell her not to go on the date. To stay with him instead.

Then he thought about how little he had to offer a woman like Tessa, who craved adventure, when his life was the antithesis of exciting.

So he didn't call for her. He simply returned to the task at hand and tried to put her out of his mind.

Tessa climbed up the hill from the hot springs later that week. She'd walked down for a dip in the water after a long day of managing her sister's media schedule because she was restless and needed something to help calm her.

They'd added two more dates to Julia's book tour, Nashville and Charleston. Tessa knew her sister had chosen those two cities because they were places Tessa wanted to visit. Julia had casually suggested they could check out the Opryland resort and the Ryman, huge on Tessa's bucket list since she loved country music.

Then Julia had requested Tessa book two nights on a nearby coastal island after the stop in Charleston. Tessa had never been to the beach, a fact her sister was well aware of. Julia wasn't playing fair by tempting Tessa to join her on the tour. But even though it would mean getting to see parts of the country she'd always wanted to visit, it also felt like Julia would be taking care of her. Watching over her.

Tessa wanted to travel on her own and choose her adventures. She had the money saved and nothing was stopping her.

Nothing but fear.

She hated being afraid of life and the fact that she couldn't seem to break herself out of the cycle of it. Yes, she was far more adventurous now than she'd been when she first arrived in Starlight. But even when she made steps in the direction of her dreams, she was still plagued by impostor syndrome.

Probably because she was an impostor. This persona she'd adopted still didn't feel like who she truly was at her core. She was beginning to question whether that wild woman was even who she truly wanted to be.

The path that led to the hot springs deposited her on the road on the far side of Carson's house. The only way to avoid walking past would have been to bushwhack her way through the thick woods.

He hadn't been home when she'd walked toward the hot springs, but now she could see his truck in the driveway along with another late model SUV parked behind it. He stood near the mailbox with a woman who looked to be a few years older than Tessa. As she got closer, she recognized Nancy Braden, the local Realtor whose banners graced the signage attached to the back of nearly every cart at the local grocery.

They were clearly engaged in an intense conversation based on the way the woman was flapping her hands in harsh contrast to Carson's ramrod-straight posture.

Tessa gave a flimsy wave as she moved past, feeling awkward, as if she'd interrupted something. Nancy called her name as she turned to glance in Tessa's direction. "Any trouble with the house?" the Realtor asked with forced cheer.

"It's all good," Tessa assured her.

"Let me know when you're ready to find a place of your own, maybe down in town. Your aunt's cabin was one of the properties that brought people to the agency's online rental site. It would be great if we got it back on the market before summer."

Tessa nodded. She didn't appreciate the reminder that she was living at the cabin thanks to her aunt's generosity. But what was the point of renting something long-term on her own if she wasn't even sure she was going to stay in Starlight?

"There's a chance I'll be traveling for the summer." The bite of Carson's gaze had her chest constricting. He looked at her as if he knew all her deepest secrets and understood she'd wanted to shock him.

Based on the way he glared, she'd succeeded.

"That's wonderful," Nancy exclaimed. "Must be nice to be so footloose and fancy-free without a care in the world."

"Footloose," Tessa repeated. "That's me. A regular Kevin Bacon over here."

"Tessa, can you help me convince Carson that he needs to let me have my way on something?" Nancy's smile turned sickeningly sweet. "I actually stopped by after showing a house farther up the mountain for a specific reason."

Carson immediately shook his head. "I've already told you my decision."

Tessa could hear the irritation in his voice and edged closer to them. She didn't particularly like Nancy but any excuse to annoy Carson was worth it in her mind.

"What's up?" She flashed him a wide grin. He didn't look happy about her potential involvement.

His gaze wandered over her, and she resisted the urge to wrap the towel she carried around her waist. She was wearing a denim shirt unbuttoned over her bathing suit top and shorts that covered her bikini bottoms. There was nothing special or remarkable about the outfit, and she'd braided her hair to keep it out of her face.

"The women's business association in town is sponsoring a Mother's Day tea this Saturday," Nancy explained. "All of the girls in Lauren's grade have RSVP'd except her."

"Because her mom isn't here," Carson said tightly.

Tessa wanted to walk away again. Irritating him

was one thing, but inserting herself into a situation that concerned his daughter was a different story. She liked Lauren and didn't appreciate the knowing gleam in Nancy's gaze, like she had this single dad and his kid all figured out.

"But I told you I'll take her." Nancy smoothed a hand over her silky blond hair. "She and my Sarabelle are friends. It's not a big deal. I'd do it for any motherless child."

Tessa made a little sound of disbelief that she tried to cover with a cough. Based on the way Carson glanced in her direction, she hadn't quite managed it.

"She's not motherless." Tessa heard the threat of tension in his tone. "Her mom just isn't here."

"I understand." Nancy was obviously trying to sound patient but not quite pulling it off. "She's traveling through Europe. Footloose and fancy-free, just like Tessa."

"Something like that," Carson agreed almost reluctantly.

Tessa had the urge to argue. She didn't want to be compared to his ex-wife.

"Why can't Carson take her?"

Nancy looked aghast. "Because it's a Mother's Day tea."

Tessa shook her head. "Surely there are other girls whose mothers might not be available that day. What about Josh's daughter?"

"Mara has stepped in to take her." Nancy said the words as if they explained everything. "Lauren has me." She reached out and squeezed Carson's bicep. Her hand lingered on his arm a few seconds longer than necessary as far as Tessa was concerned.

"I see Carson's point," she said, earning a frown from Nancy. "It would be strange for a different mother to take her to this tea. She has a mother who just can't be here. Maybe if there were a family friend or her babysitter…"

"You could take her," Carson said suddenly. Both Nancy and Tessa stared at him for several long moments.

"I don't think that's a great idea." Nancy sounded even more irritated. "I'm not sure why she'd be any more appropriate than me."

"Lauren likes Tessa. She'd feel comfortable with her."

Tessa continued to stare at him. She couldn't believe he'd volunteered her for this role when it seemed like just yesterday that he was warning her away from his daughter.

Nancy gave Tessa another judgy once-over. "I suppose that would be okay. We've had grandmothers and aunts at the event in the past. But this is a classy event. Refined."

Tessa reached up and made a show of scratching her right breast. "Oh, trust me." She pretended to snap gum that she wasn't actually chewing. "I'm quite refined."

Nancy sighed and looked at Carson again. "Are you sure you wouldn't rather have me bring Lauren?"

"Tessa's got this."

"Well, I'll bring over some of Sarabelle's old dresses tomorrow. She said Lauren doesn't own anything but leggings."

"Okay…well…" Carson looked like he didn't quite know how to answer.

"I'll take her shopping," Tessa offered. "She does have dresses at her mom's house. Because let's remember, Nanc, that this girl isn't motherless. There's no reason to go all *Little Orphan Annie* on the situation. They are working it out like single parents do when they're co-parenting. Give it a rest."

"I'm trying to be helpful." Nancy spoke through gritted teeth.

"Appreciated. As is your reminder that my aunt could bring in a lot more money with the cabin as a short-term rental. I'll give you a call if we need anything."

"Great." The other woman stalked to her car and backed out onto the road. As soon as she was down the hill and out of sight, Lauren came running through the front door.

"Hey, Daddy, did you tell Sarabelle's mom that I can go to the Mother's Day thing with them? I know it's kind of weird 'cause Mom isn't here but all my friends are going and Sarabelle said I could borrow a dress."

"Tessa offered to take you," Carson told his daughter. Although Tessa taking Lauren was Carson's idea, he didn't sound happy about it.

"That's awesome." Lauren gave Tessa a tight hug around the waist. "Will you do my hair, too?"

"Of course, and your dad asked if I would take you shopping for a new dress for the event." Lauren's wide eyes grew even bigger.

"A new dress?" she whispered. "Daddy, I'm gonna pick out the prettiest one." She transferred the hug to Carson, and Tessa's heart melted as his broad shoulders relaxed.

"Baby, you could wear a paper sack and you'd be the prettiest girl I know."

Thank you, he mouthed to Tessa. With a quick wave, she headed up the road toward her house, wishing she knew how to keep Carson and Lauren from running away with her heart.

Chapter Twelve

Carson sat on the sofa in Tessa's family room the following Saturday morning, doing his best not to fidget. He felt as nervous as an awkward teenager picking up a girl for his first high school dance.

This morning the girl in question was his daughter, and he was waiting to see her before she and Tessa left for their event. The two of them had gone shopping, along with a couple of Tessa's friends, at some bridal boutique in the next town over, which terrified Carson probably more than it should. His daughter had returned with two dresses and an invitation to Cory and Jordan's wedding.

He hadn't been a guest at a wedding in years, but

Lauren was so darn excited about the prospect there was no chance of him saying no. She had refused to show him either dress, telling him she wanted it to be a surprise for each event. She'd walked down to Tessa's cabin an hour earlier to get ready.

This was a part of parenting a girl that he could never hope to master. He wasn't going to learn about hairstyles and fashion and could only hope that his ex-wife would come to her senses and return home once the party on tour was over.

Unfortunately, that would bring a whole host of new issues, namely how Carson would handle it if Delilah did return and decided to move back to the Southeast. He felt confident he could find a job anywhere, but he liked Starlight. Even without the undeniable attraction to Tessa, he liked the town and the people. Carson's dad had been career military so he'd gotten used to moving around as a kid. He hadn't realized he'd care about staying in one place but things were changing. He was changing.

He heard whispers from the back hall, and then Tessa called out, "Presenting Miss Lauren Nicole Campbell."

Carson quickly stood and wiped his palms off on the denim of his jeans. He turned as his daughter made her way slowly around the corner and into the room. She looked nearly as nervous as he felt. A dull ache settled in his chest at the thought of how much time he'd lost with her and whether he'd ever truly be able to regain her trust and love. But mainly his heart throbbed at the sight of her beauty and the pride she obviously felt at being dressed up for the occasion.

The dress she'd chosen was pale yellow with a frilly lace overlay and a bow at the collar. Her hair was up in some kind of intricate knot with tendrils curling around her face. She was the perfect mix of his sweet baby and the gorgeous young woman she was no doubt going to grow into.

"Do the twirl," Tessa stage-whispered from the hallway.

Lauren giggled and took two steps forward then reached out her arms to either side and executed two fast circles, her dress spinning around her.

"You are beautiful." He walked toward her then remembered to grab the box of flowers Tessa had instructed him to retrieve from the refrigerator when he'd arrived at the house. "You are beautiful every day, baby girl, but that dress is exquisite."

She grinned so hard. "I'm like a princess."

Carson didn't have any experience with princesses or understand why young girls were so fascinated by them, but he nodded in agreement.

"What's that, Daddy?" She pointed to the box.

"A corsage to go with your dress." He opened the box and took out the wristlet. "If you want to wear it."

"I do. I feel so happy. I wish Mommy was here to see me. She likes dressing up."

The ache returned. "We'll take lots of pictures and text them to your mom. Maybe next year she'll be able to go to the event with you."

Lauren inclined her head. "Do you think Mommy will come back and move to Starlight with us?"

Wow. There was a conversation he didn't expect to have when his emotions were already pinging around like a ball shot into a pinball machine. "We'll have to see, but right now let's focus on you having a great time at the tea."

"I hope they have lots of little pastries," Tessa said.

Carson glanced up and his breath whooshed out of his lungs.

He wasn't sure what he'd expected Tessa to wear for her stand-in role at the mother-daughter tea, especially after she'd seemed to take so much joy in giving Nancy the business.

Mentally, Carson had prepared himself for anything. Leopard print miniskirt or a tank top with leather fringe. One thing he did not count on was Tessa wearing a demure floral-print dress with a sash at the waist and a tiny ruffle around the hem, her red curls smoothed into tame waves that fell around her shoulders.

Instead of the dark makeup she normally favored,

she wore a soft pink gloss on her lips and maybe a little blush. Or maybe she had a full face of makeup on but had applied it so subtly that he couldn't tell. She looked like she would fit in at the snobbiest society event. She would turn the mothers of Starlight inside out with jealousy.

It was ridiculous but Carson felt jealous of whatever man would end up with a woman like her. A bundle of contradictions but a person with enough class and generosity of spirit to put aside her personal feelings and make it the perfect day for a girl who'd been through too much uncertainty in her life.

"You look nice," he said then quickly added, "Beautiful. You both look beautiful."

"Did you get Tessa flowers, too?" Lauren was still admiring her corsage and oblivious to the awareness rippling between the two adults in the room.

"I don't need flowers." Tessa's cheeks colored in that familiar shade of pink Carson was coming to expect. "We should go so we're not late."

"I'll take lots of pictures and send them to you," she told Carson.

It took him a moment to register her words. He was legitimately stunned by her beauty, both inside and out.

"Right. Thanks. I'm heading into town myself. Josh invited a few guys to Trophy Room for wings.

Do you want me to drive you? We can all ride down together."

"Sure," Tessa said softly. "Thanks."

As they loaded up in Carson's truck, he realized how normal this seemed and how right. Which made him even more certain that it couldn't last.

Tessa's phone beeped where it sat on her nightstand later that evening. She grabbed it and read the text from Carson.

Are you awake? Come to the front door.

She padded out from her bedroom in her pajamas and opened the door of the cabin to reveal him standing there with a bouquet of flowers in his hand.

He wore a sweatshirt and faded jeans and looked about as irresistible as any man she'd ever seen. So unfair.

"Sorry to bother you. I know it's late."

"A man holding a bouquet of flowers is never a bother," she said with a nervous laugh. There was something about the quiet hour and the darkness surrounding them that felt particularly intimate. More likely it was her now-familiar reaction to Carson that made her nervous and with good reason. He made her want things she didn't even know how to articulate—more than just experience and adventure. He made her want more in every area.

"Thank you for today," he said, thrusting the blooms in her direction. "Lauren had the most amazing time, and the corsage was a great touch. I wouldn't have even thought to think of that."

"I went to a father-daughter dance one time, and my dad got me flowers. It made me feel special, which was nice since it was the only dance I ever went to."

Carson let out a soft sigh. "I should have guessed you were one of those."

"One of what?" she asked as she studied the delicate flowers. They were a mix of tulips and lilies, a perfect spring blend and one that made her think of new life, renewal and fresh starts.

"The kids who didn't actually show up at the dance because they were too busy partying. I knew girls like you in high school. Heck, I dated girls like you in high school."

She let out a soft laugh. "Boys like you did not date girls like me in high school. I wasn't skipping dances because I was busy partying, Carson. Things got bad with my health in high school. I spent most of my time in the hospital. There was no partying or dances. By that point, I'd passed out a couple of times at school. My classmates were terrified of me.

Thought you could catch kidney disease or something along those lines."

"I'm sorry," he said. "If things were difficult and kept you out of commission, when did this rebellious streak start?"

"Oh, I don't know. I like to think I was always a bit of a closet rebel."

"Is that so?" One side of his mouth curved into a smile that sent Tessa's hormones into overdrive. The guy was too tempting for her own good. It was late and just the two of them were there in the darkness. He might not want her to be the rebel but he believed her to be one. So she leaned forward and fused her mouth to his.

Part of her expected him to push her away. To be smarter than her. Maybe he was sick of doing the right thing, too. Because he didn't hesitate to wrap his arms around her and lift her off her feet. She curled her legs around his hips as he backed into the cabin and kicked the door shut with one foot. She'd seen that move in movies but had never imagined she'd be part of a scene like this.

And what a scene it was. He kissed her like he couldn't get enough. She dropped the bouquet on the entry table as his tongue melded with hers and lost all sense of time and place until her shoulder brushed the side of a doorframe. The door to her bedroom.

Oh, Lord. This was happening. She wanted it,

there was no doubt. Still, nerves flooded her. As he lowered her to the bed, Carson's kisses gentled and slowed.

"Do you want to stop?" he asked, and Tessa realized with complete certainty that she didn't want to stop. No matter what came next, she wanted this moment with this man.

"I want to see you," she said, barely recognizing the husky note in her tone.

Carson didn't seem surprised by it as he nodded. "Yes," he murmured.

He straightened and tore off his shirt then pushed down his pants and boxer briefs. That was when Tessa would have expected the nerves to return, but they didn't.

All she felt was a deep yearning.

"That's impressive," she said, glancing up into his face again.

He chuckled. "We haven't even gotten started with the ways I'm planning to impress you."

Need exploded through her. She was almost afraid for him to touch her, because she wasn't sure she could stand the pleasure of it. What if she actually came apart before things even got started?

After sheathing himself with a condom, he lowered to the bed and explored her mouth for several blissful minutes before trailing kisses along her throat. He pushed back and lifted her shirt up and over her head.

"Wait."

He immediately stilled.

Tessa squeezed shut her eyes. "I know it's already kind of dark in here, but could you close the blinds?" She pointed toward the window, still keeping her eyes closed.

"Why?" Carson's voice was laced with amusement. "If I had my way, I'd light up the room like the Fourth of July so I could see you, Tessa. All of you."

"That's kind of the problem." She forced herself to meet his gaze. "My body…"

"Is beautiful," he supplied.

"Not quite. I have scars, Carson. A lot of them. I don't want to freak you out. In fact, if we could just make my torso a no-touch zone, that would be awesome. Thank you very much."

"Can't do that."

"Sure you can. Heck, not much happens in that area."

"Tessa." He shifted so that he was lying next to her.

No, she wanted to scream. Now she'd done it. She'd ruined the moment with her insecurities and pointing out what was wrong with her. There were so many that weren't even visible to the eye, but now he would pay more attention to her most obvious flaws.

"Your scars don't scare me. They make you who you are. I want to be with you right now. All of you."

She dragged in a shaky breath. She was at risk of losing control of her heart as much as her body when he said things like that. Dangerous things. Things she wanted to believe.

But two words stuck out. *Right now.* She swallowed. That was the reminder she needed. Whatever happened in this moment wasn't about anything long-term. There were no promises or vows between them. It was only right now, and she could manage at least that much.

"In that case…" She tried to put a teasing note into her voice. No sense really scaring him off. "I'm ready to be impressed."

Carson kissed her again then moved down her body, his mouth hot and sure on her skin. He cupped her breasts and kissed each pebbled nipple, and she couldn't have stopped the needy groan that escaped her lips for all the money in the world. She arched into him without even realizing what she was doing, and when he peeled down her pajama shorts and panties, Tessa was too far gone with need and desire to feel a flush of embarrassment.

She could sense his eyes on her body and something different in the feel of him as he claimed her mouth again. He teased and tortured her with his fingers until she felt like she might lose her mind.

"Please," she whispered as he settled himself between her legs. He entered her in one fluid stroke.

It's what she'd been waiting for, but the sensation still took her by surprise. She sucked in a breath at the flash of pain.

Carson stopped moving. "Tessa?"

"It's good," she told him, which wasn't quite a lic. As her body adjusted to his size, the initial pain was quickly being replaced by a deeper sensation. A feeling of more that was so right.

He still didn't move, however, and she was terrified that he might call her out on what she hadn't revealed and stop what they were doing. She did not want this moment to end. She might not be as seasoned as she pretended, but she knew something was missing. Something they could only find together.

She tilted her hips forward and placed her hands on his hips. "Please," she said again, unsure of what she was even asking.

Thankfully, Carson knew. He began to move in a slow steady rhythm and sensation whirled through her. Her eyes drifted shut in blissful surrender, and when she opened them again, Carson was watching her intently. She didn't know what he was looking for, so she wound her arms around his neck and pulled him closer.

As they moved together, Tessa kissed him again, and it heightened the pleasure to peaks she didn't realize she could achieve without shattering. She closed her eyes again and focused on her ragged breath as pressure built inside of her. When it crashed around her like a tidal wave, she cried out Carson's name.

He held her tighter, if that were possible, and moments later followed her over the edge of desire.

They lay in the quiet of her room for several minutes as their breathing returned to normal and Tessa worked to get her emotions under control. It felt as though her heart might burst from the joy of this moment.

"You're smiling," he said softly, one finger reaching out to trace her lips.

"Like I said, you're impressive."

"That goes both ways." He leaned in and dropped a quick kiss on her shoulder. "That was amazing and…um…it seemed like…did I hurt you?"

"No," she said immediately and rolled to the side. She grabbed her pajama shirt and underpants from the floor. "It's been a while. Kind of a dry spell in Starlight, you know?"

"Sure," he agreed, although he didn't sound nearly as convinced as she would have liked.

Chapter Thirteen

Carson stood in an alcove facing the main drag of downtown Starlight as he disconnected the call with his ex-wife Friday morning. He immediately punched his fist into the brick exterior of Main Street Perk, the town's popular coffeehouse. Just as quickly, he let out a hissed curse and painful breath at his stupidity on several different fronts.

"What are you doing?"

He glanced up as Tessa hurried toward him. He'd been on his way to Main Street Perk when his phone rang and had ducked into the quiet, shadowed space to get a modicum of privacy in case the call with

Delilah went badly. It had been worse than he could have imagined.

"You know you aren't actually Superman, right?" Tessa took his hand between hers and studied his now-bloody knuckles. "You can't go around punching brick walls and think it's going to turn out well."

He blew out another shaky breath. "It feels like it can't go any worse right now."

"You need a Band-Aid or something," she said. "Let's go into the shop and—"

"I'm fine." Even though her touch felt exquisitely good, he forced himself to pull his hand away. He didn't want to take comfort right now. He didn't want to feel better but needed to be angry, and bitter, and wallowing in the mess of his life.

"What's going on?" The concern in her tone nearly undid him, although not as much as the memory of their time together and the fact that he wanted more of it. "I'm grabbing muffins before meeting my friends, and I see you doing the Mike Tyson routine. You'll never win against a wall, Carson."

He'd seen her several times this week. She'd even come to soccer practice at Lauren's urging. But Tessa wasn't his girlfriend. She was his neighbor who he'd slept with and that was damn irresponsible for a single father, especially when she was his daughter's favorite person in town. She was his favorite person in town as well, and he didn't want to take a chance on ruining it, but that didn't change him wanting her.

He wanted her far more than he should.

"I just got off the phone with Delilah."

"Lauren's mom?"

"The other night before they FaceTimed, I sent her the photos of Lauren from the tea." Lauren had been so excited to tell her mom all about the fancy event she'd attended.

"Is that a bad thing?"

"Not exactly. Not for normal parents. The kind that are happy when their kids are happy. Delilah likes to be the center of attention. She takes great pride in it and the fact that her daughter is happy and she's not here…well, that doesn't seem to be going over very well." He sighed and scrubbed a hand over his face. "She's flying into Seattle next week because there's a short break in the tour schedule. She said she wants to talk about the future."

"Do you think that means she's coming back for Lauren?"

"I stopped second-guessing Delilah's thought patterns years ago, but that's my fear. It was like she was happier when Lauren was unhappy, which is twisted."

"Well, then, you'll fight for her," Tessa said as if there was no question.

He wished he felt half as confident. "You're right," he agreed because what else could he do? And there was no question that he'd take whatever steps necessary to continue to be a part of Lauren's life and not just on holidays or weekends. He wanted as much time with her as he could get. The little moments. Even when he didn't know what he was doing and that was often, he still wanted the chance to try.

"When are you going to the city? If you need to miss the wedding—"

"No way. Lauren is so excited about the wedding. I'm going to keep her home from school to drive into Seattle on Tuesday, and I'll get a hotel while she spends the night with her mom. Delilah has a flight to London later this week. It will be a short trip so maybe that's a silver lining."

"I have to be in the city Tuesday afternoon," Tessa said. "Routine doctor's appointment. Let me know if you need anything."

He reached out and took one of her coppery waves between his fingers. "Would you drive up with us? Stay with me Tuesday night. That's what I need, Tessa." He had no right to ask, but he didn't want to be alone and spend the whole night thinking about how badly he and Delilah had messed up with their daughter.

Tessa bit down on her lower lip, and he stifled a groan. "It sounds like you just need a distraction."

He would have agreed, but there was no point in lying. It was more than that. "I need you."

She gave a small nod. "Sure. It'll be fun. I'll even let you take me out to a nice dinner."

"I appreciate your generosity," he said with a chuckle. He went to rub his knuckle against the side of her cheek but pulled back at the last second. He'd forgotten that he was bleeding.

"You need to clean that up."

He nodded. "I'm heading home right now. I've got some paperwork to fill out before my next flight."

Madison called to them from across the street. "What kind of nefarious goings-on are happening over there? This town can't take anything that's beyond PG-rated."

Tessa let out a strangled laugh. "G-rated," she called. "You know what a Boy Scout we've got with this one."

Carson waved to Madison and asked, just loud enough for Tessa to hear, "Do I need to impress you again?"

He was rewarded when she whimpered softly. "We're heading over to start setting up at the reception venue. I'll catch you later."

"You will," he promised.

Tessa pulled into Carson's driveway a half hour later. She grabbed the bag from the pharmacy that sat on the passenger seat and then approached the door, knocking softly. Carson's eyes widened in surprise as he answered.

"What happened to working on decorations for the reception?"

Nerves jiggled through her and she wondered if he might sense that her legs felt like Jell-O. "I told them I had an unexpected call to take with my sister. Most of the work is done anyway."

"You lied to your friends." One corner of his mouth quirked.

"I was worried about your hand." She held up the bag of supplies. "I brought hydrogen peroxide and extra bandages."

He stretched out his fingers. "Taken care of. I used liquid bandages for them."

"All right. I guess you're all good here. I should go and deal with that make-believe phone call."

"Oh, no." He stretched out his hand and curled it around the back of her neck, massaging gently. "There are other parts of me that could use your attention if you're interested?"

Tessa all but melted in his arms as the door closed behind her. She knew what was coming, the end goal for something like this. Afternoon delight, as the old song would have it.

But Carson seemed in no hurry to get to the main event. He kissed her with a tenderness that should have surprised her but didn't. He was a man who had plenty of hard edges but also a soft core like gooey melted chocolate.

She'd seen it in his relationship with Lauren and now felt it in the way he held her in his arms as they moved up the stairs toward his bedroom.

She didn't know the man he'd been when he was younger but had a suspicion his ex-wife was a complete idiot. How could anybody give up a man like this? Tessa knew he wasn't truly for her, but she was going to take advantage of and appreciate every moment they had together.

They shed their clothes and explored each other's bodies for minutes—or maybe hours—and this time when he entered her, there was no pain. Only a deep sense of it being right—and not just physically. They fit together perfectly in a way she couldn't quite understand.

She'd come to Starlight to change her life. She wanted to learn to take risks and to have adventures, to rebel against the staid and boring life she'd known. She was quickly coming to understand that real change wasn't going to happen from things like wearing different makeup or skinny-dipping in a hot spring. The change she was experiencing now came from inside of her. A deep need to take true risks to become the person she wanted to be.

And she might not expect that shift to take place in this stubborn man's arms, but it was happening nonetheless.

As Carson waited for Tessa in the lobby of the sterile medical office, it felt as though his skin was two sizes too small for his body.

He'd dropped Lauren off to Delilah, and his sweet daughter had been ecstatic for the reunion with her mom. He felt like the world's biggest jerk for his jealousy. He wanted his daughter to have a great relationship with her mother. And for his ex-wife to be the kind of mom that Lauren needed.

But a nagging fear kept creeping in like a noxious weed—the fear that if Delilah stepped up, it wouldn't leave room for him. At least not in the full-time way he'd gotten used to. He didn't want to be relegated to the sidelines again.

He also understood he would do whatever was best for his kid.

With that came the realization that he hadn't done his best by her for too long now. Her entire life up until the move to Starlight. He could easily hate himself for it.

He glanced around the waiting room of the nephrology practice, which was filled with patients of various ages. He rarely went to the doctor and couldn't imagine how Tessa had managed it growing up. She didn't like to talk about her surgeries or the health problems she'd dealt with leading up to the transplant.

Carson couldn't help his curiosity. He'd tried not to stare at the web of scars on her abdomen, not because it bothered him but out of respect for the way it seemed to make her feel. For all her tough talk and sass, her body told a much more compelling story about her strength and resilience than anything else.

He'd done some research on kidney transplant

patients, and his admiration for Tessa had grown exponentially. He wanted to know more about her background and to understand what she'd been through and what had brought her to this place.

It was doubtful she'd be willing to share that information, and he also doubted that his curiosity was smart for either of them. She'd mentioned a possible plan to leave Starlight this summer and then join her famous sister on the book tour. When Carson had asked her about it, she'd refused to discuss details.

Her relationship with Julia was complicated. He understood complicated relationships. He'd grown up as the third of six kids who'd been born within an eight-year time span. His father was career military, dedicated to his country and his family but gruff and unsure of how to give affection other than in the form of rigid structure. Carson's mom had been on her own with the kids a lot, and the six of them had definitely given her a run for her money.

His parents had done the best they could. There'd been a lot of work and mouths to feed and not much time for outward displays of love or personal attention. It's the way Carson had been raised, and he hadn't exactly known how to do any different until Tessa had shown him. She'd been particularly helpful with assisting him in managing his feelings around his daughter's asthma.

At first, his inclination had been to treat Lauren

like a delicate flower. He'd been terrified by knowing the way her lungs contracted and seeing her cough and wheeze during an attack. To him, the best way to handle it was to make sure she was never exposed to a situation that put her in danger of having an issue. Tessa had helped him understand he couldn't keep Lauren in a bubble.

If she wanted to do something like play soccer, they could manage that. Tessa helped him research an asthma action plan and talk to Lauren's teammates about her condition and how it wasn't anything to be scared of.

He got the impression that no one had helped Tessa live an active life as a child. Although her issues might have been more debilitating than asthma, the principle was the same. She hadn't felt like she could participate the way she wanted to, and it influenced her decisions even now.

Working at the Thirsty Chicken was a perfect example. That job didn't sit well with Carson even though he trusted her judgment and knew she could rely on her coworkers to take care of her as best they could. However, he'd learned quickly that she wasn't going to be told what to do by anyone, especially not him. He respected her for that. He respected her and he was damn attracted to her, although he wished he had a better control over how often he thought about her as he went through his day.

He liked talking to her and making her laugh. He enjoyed listening to her unique take on things and watching the way she interacted with his daughter.

The cynical part of him inwardly shouted that he should get up and walk out of this waiting room right now before she came out. Put a little space between them. Great sex was one thing but really opening himself up to her when both of their futures were so uncertain was emotional suicide.

"What are you doing here?"

He shifted in his chair to see Tessa glaring at him as the door from the lobby to the exam rooms closed behind her.

"I thought we were going to meet back at the hotel."

He suddenly realized he wasn't the only one worried about maintaining boundaries and living behind the safety of the walls he'd created. While he didn't mind those walls in himself, hers he wanted to break down. She wasn't like him. Her nature was sweet and caring. She had an immense amount of love to give if she could find a way to trust herself to do it.

At least he could help with that if nothing else. "I didn't have much going on today so figured I could offer you a ride. How was your appointment?"

Her eyes went even more guarded. "Fine. Everything is fine."

"Miss Reynolds? I've got the reminder paperwork

for your next visit and the lab orders. The doctor will want you to get in right away so he can review the results."

Tessa hurried forward and grabbed the business card the woman held out. "Got it. Thank you."

No one else in the waiting room paid her a bit of attention, but Carson could see she was upset. His stomach clenched in response to her obvious mood. What had happened in the appointment today? What did the doctor tell her? Did he even have a right to ask?

His worries about Delilah seemed to pale in comparison. No matter what his ex-wife wanted or her reasons for coming back right now, he could deal with it. He could take care of Lauren.

Who would take care of Tessa if she needed it? He followed her out into the warm sunshine of the Seattle afternoon.

A breeze whistled through the trees and the scent of freshly cut grass tickled his nose. Summer was nearly upon them. Would Tessa take off to join her sister on the book tour?

"Was it hard to change doctors from whoever you went to back in Cleveland?" he asked, figuring that was an innocent question.

"It's fine. You didn't need to come and get me. I'm plenty capable of making my way to the hotel."

"I know. I wanted to see you."

"You just left me a couple of hours ago." She climbed into the car when he unlocked it. "There was no need for this. Unless…oh, wait. Are we going to park someplace and have a quickie in the back seat? Is that it? Get the most out of your time without Lauren?"

He knew she was trying to hurt him with her words and damn if they didn't hit the mark.

He turned on the truck but didn't pull out of the lot right away. "Using sex as a weapon," he said, arching an eyebrow in her direction. "That's original."

Her lips thinned but she didn't respond.

"Just so we're clear, it was a real kick in the teeth to drop off my daughter with my ex. I came here instead of meeting you at the hotel because I didn't want to be alone. More than not wanting to be alone, I wanted to be with you. That's what I'm doing here, Tessa. If we don't have sex at all today or tomorrow or ever again…well, that will be a damn shame but it won't stop me from wanting to hang out with you. It's not just about the physical part for me, although it would be a lot easier if it were."

He watched as she drew in a shaky breath but continued to stare straight ahead and remained silent. He understood he'd taken a chance by showing up at her doctor's office but hadn't realized what a mistake it would be.

"I'll drop you off at the hotel," he said as he put

the truck into Drive. "I can find some way to entertain myself this afternoon and if you need more time alone, I'll get a different room."

"My blood pressure was high and there's some tenderness around the area where the transplant was done," she said quietly. "It might not be a big deal, but the new doctor wants to change up my meds and monitor things more closely. I've gotten to the point where I see myself as somebody healthy. I was starting to, anyway. That's what coming to Starlight was about, you know. Me becoming a new person. The person I couldn't be when I was the sick girl with kidney disease. I can't get away from it. Not when it follows me. Not when it's part of me. I just want to be normal."

A laugh popped out of him at those words, and she swatted him on the arm. "That's rude."

He reached across the console and took her hand. She tried to tug it away, but he held fast. "It's not meant to be a criticism, sweetheart. But you could never be normal. You are special and unique and absolutely one of a kind. Not because of the kidney disease or the fact that you were sick or anything outside of you. You're special because of who you are on the inside. There's no point in trying to pretend anything else. I'm sorry you got news you didn't want, but I know you're strong enough to handle it. I'm glad I'm here even if you don't want me here."

She squeezed his fingers. It was gentle, but he knew it meant something.

"I do want you here. It scares me how much I want you here."

"That makes two of us. I guess it's okay to be scared together."

"Scared together," she repeated with a smile. "Aren't we a pair?"

Chapter Fourteen

It was a testament to how much Tessa liked being with Carson and his effect on her that her mood had improved by the time they had dinner that night.

They'd returned to the hotel. She'd talked to her mom and did her best not to cry. Tessa had downplayed the additional tests the doctor had ordered, and her mom's tone had stayed positive as she offered words of encouragement and assurances that everything would work out.

She'd also offered to come and stay with Tessa when she went for the follow-up appointment, but Tessa had refused. She was an adult now and she would handle things on her own. That's what she'd wanted, right? To be grown-up and independent, able to take care of herself and not to need anyone.

In the end, her mom had agreed not to schedule a flight after Tessa promised to call if she started feeling tired or developed a fever. She'd begged her mom not to put her dad on the phone, unsure whether she'd be able to talk to him without breaking down. If her body rejected the kidney he'd given her, the guilt would be almost more than she could handle. True to his word, Carson had given her time alone, even though she wasn't at all sure that's what she wanted or needed from him.

She told herself it was for the best because if she let herself depend on him, it would certainly end in disaster. At least for her heart.

After hanging up with her mom, she'd curled up in a ball and fallen asleep on top of the comforter, only to wake when Carson returned to the room and covered her with a thin blanket.

It had taken no thought at all for her to reach up and pull him down with her. She'd been a jerk earlier when he'd clearly been hurting after dropping off Lauren to her mom. It wasn't fair of Tessa to take out her frustrations on him, but she didn't know how to explain the mix of fear and disappointment warring inside her. She'd tried to show him with her body what she wasn't able to say out loud. That he meant something to her. They'd made love quietly…slowly, each of them giving and taking in turn as they discovered more about each other's needs and desires.

After, he'd carried her into the shower. The release and his quiet ministrations had been exactly what she'd needed to revive and rejuvenate, and she'd emerged feeling like she could face whatever came next.

They'd napped, made love again and then headed out for dinner. He'd chosen a downtown restaurant with a view of the water, and they sat at a table overlooking Puget Sound.

"It's like we're on a real date," she told him as the waiter delivered a crème brûlée with two spoons to the table to finish off the meal.

Carson gave her a quizzical look. "You mean it isn't a real date?"

"No. We aren't a couple. We're neighbors."

"Who happen to have the best sex of our lives together," he added. "And go out to dinner together."

"We have to eat." She pointed a finger at him. "Go back to that best-sex-of-your-life part. Is that true?"

"Hell, yeah." He took a small sip of his water. "Don't tell me I'm the only one because it would crush my ego if I thought you'd had better."

"I haven't," she said quietly. "Actually, I haven't had any."

"Right, the dry spell."

"I wasn't exactly honest about that, Carson."

His thick brows drew together. "What do you mean you weren't honest about that? Are you saying there wasn't a dry spell?"

Oh, why did she have to feel the need to be honest at this moment? They'd had such a good date and he had the best sex of his life with her. Why hadn't she kept her mouth shut? "Let's talk about something else. Forget I said anything."

He placed his spoon from the crème brûlée on the table and leaned forward. "Are you sleeping with other men while you're sleeping with me?"

Tessa sucked in a breath at his question. Should she laugh or be offended that he thought she would do something so brazen? Offended seemed like a stretch since this was exactly what she wanted him to think about her...

She wished she were some sort of wild, carefree rebel but the reality of it and the way he was looking at her didn't add up to how she thought it would feel to be seen that way.

"Tessa, answer me. I was very clear with you that monogamy is important to me. I have to be careful. I have a daughter. I have—"

"I was a virgin," she blurted and then realized that the waiter had returned to their table with the check.

"I'll just leave this here," the young man said, careful not to make eye contact with either of them.

He placed the black folder on the table while Tessa silently prayed for the ground to swallow her whole.

Once again she'd made a complete idiot of herself in front of Carson. She could have stayed quiet or she could have let him think she was sleeping with half of Starlight.

Either option seemed like it would have been better than the way he was looking at her like she'd just grown a unicorn horn out of her forehead.

"So when I say it wasn't exactly a dry spell I mean because I wasn't having sex with anybody." As if he didn't know what the word *virgin* meant. "Stop staring at me and say something. I'm embarrassed enough as it is."

"Why are you embarrassed?" He flicked a glance toward the door that led to the restaurant's kitchen. "Other than the fact that you just announced it to the waiter."

"Well, that seems like a fairly good reason. I'm embarrassed because I'm too old to be a virgin."

"You're not a virgin," he pointed out. "We've had sex several times now."

"Does this make you change your mind about thinking it was the best sex of your life?"

"Why would that change anything?"

"Because I told you I was experienced. You thought you were with somebody who knew what they were doing."

He breathed out a soft laugh. "Tessa, if you had affected me any more than you did, I might not have made it out alive. The only reason I care about your experience or lack of experience or whatever you want to call it is that I would have tried to make it better for you if I had known. God."

He shook his head. "Did I hurt you? I don't even remember thinking about being careful. I was just so caught up in the moment and —"

"You were careful enough," she told him. The last thing she wanted to do was make him feel bad, not when he made her feel so good. "I might not have a ton of experience, but I know how things are supposed to work. Between us they worked really, really well."

His mouth curved up. "They did. Tessa, I'm honored that you chose me for your first time."

"And my second and third," she reminded him. "What are we on now…"

"I'm not counting. This isn't…you weren't a feather in my cap. I'm attracted to you. I like you."

"Even though you don't want to like me or trust me with your daughter."

"About that." He ran a hand over his jaw. "All of this big talk about you being a rebel and doing terrible things and your irresponsibility. How much of that is true?"

She squirmed under his scrutiny. "That's a hard

question to answer. There's the me I've been for my whole life and then there's the person I want to be. I don't want to think about the scared, sick girl who never had a boyfriend or any experience or any adventure or any fun. I don't want to be that person."

"You aren't that person. Not anymore. But I'm also not sure you're the person you're pretending to be. Pretending is a lot of work."

"Tell me about it," she muttered.

"I'm trying to."

"Well, that's why I told you the truth. I want you to know the real me. I'm not quite as much fun as you're probably used to."

"I've had a lot of fun with you. In fact, I intend to have a lot more fun with you tonight."

She bit down on her lip as anticipation curled through her. Part of her had worried that by sharing the truth, she'd chase him away. The way he was looking at her told a totally different story. One she couldn't wait to read more of.

Carson's cell phone vibrated where he placed it on the table. "Let me just make sure. Damn. It's Delilah. I need to take it." He accepted the call and lifted the phone to his ear. "Hello. Lauren? Where are you, baby?… Where is your mom? What's going on?… No, no it's fine… Yeah, you were right to call me. I'm sure it's good. You stay where you are in the bathroom… Nope. It doesn't matter who's knocking on the door. Unless your mom comes back before I get there you don't answer it for anybody."

He stood as he was speaking, pulled out his wallet and threw a stack of bills on the table. "My phone is almost out of battery, Laur." He muttered a curse. "If I lose you, stay exactly where you are and don't let anyone into the bathroom. I'll be there as soon as I can."

Tessa had to jog to keep up with him as he strode from the restaurant. "What's going on?" she asked as he punched the face of his cell phone with one angry finger.

"Delilah had people back to the hotel. She told Lauren she was going to grab a candy bar and she hasn't come back. My daughter is in a hotel room with a party going on and her mother is nowhere to be found."

He held the phone up to his ear again. "Hi, I'm in room 1604. The room next to me sounds like they're having a pretty wild party. Could you send somebody up to settle things down? Thanks."

He was practically sprinting now, and Tessa took off her wedge heels and padded barefoot next to him so she could keep up. "Why didn't you tell them about Lauren in the bathroom?"

"I don't want to admit that my daughter is at a hotel with no parental supervision and a bunch of random adults. What if the people at the front desk decide to call the cops? We're only a couple of blocks away. If she's locked in and they're going up to check on the room, that should give me enough time to get there."

"It gives *us* enough time," Tessa corrected. "I'm in this with you, Carson. Whatever you need."

"I need to get to my daughter."

Carson tried not to flinch as Tessa took his hand later that night in the hallway outside the room where his daughter had finally fallen asleep.

By the time he'd gotten to Delilah's hotel room, she'd returned, mad as a hornet that he'd sent the front desk to break up the party with her friends.

A small get-together, she'd called it, with people she trusted.

It hadn't mattered that their daughter had been terrified. Lauren had emerged from the bathroom with her face pale as ash but dry of tears. She'd been clutching her inhaler, and Carson knew stress was one of her triggers for an asthma attack. The guilt that washed over him had been sure and swift, like a raging mountain river after a season of rain.

He'd been enjoying himself while Lauren had been scared and alone. Maybe if Tessa hadn't come on the trip with them he would have gotten a room at the same hotel as Delilah. Maybe it wouldn't have taken those extra minutes to get to his daughter.

But as he stood in that hotel room facing down his ex-wife, he'd wanted Tessa at his side.

That hadn't happened because she'd left him at the elevator. He hadn't wanted to set off Delilah. It would if she knew he'd been with a woman in the city. Tessa had returned to their hotel to book a second room for Carson and Lauren.

"It might be fun," Tessa said now. "Nashville is a great city."

"But how long will that last?" he asked, not really expecting her to answer. "What happens when they break up or he's ready to tour again? Or she meets somebody else?"

After Delilah's friends had gone, Lauren watched TV and snuggled in the bed while her parents talked. Delilah had let Carson in on the news that at the end of the tour, her fiancé, Robbie, and his band were heading to Nashville because they wanted to record a country album. She wanted Lauren to move to Tennessee with them. Carson didn't know much about British rockers, but it didn't sound like the best idea he'd ever heard and not one that was suited to give his daughter the kind of homelife he wanted for her.

"Well," Tessa said, her voice carefully neutral, "I'd think with a new baby that things would be somewhat stable."

He appreciated her attempt at finding a silver lining in this situation, but he also doubted Delilah's pregnancy would be a positive change.

"Nashville," he said again. "I don't want to move to Nashville."

Tessa slipped her hand from his. "But you will."

"Delilah wants Lauren with her."

"After tonight…"

"I can't not be where my kid is, and not just because my ex-wife has gone off the deep end. She wasn't like this before the new guy." He scrubbed a hand over his face. "At least I don't think she was. Lauren always seemed fine and happy when I saw her. How much have I been missing?"

"You're a great dad."

"I don't know about that, but I'm trying." He sent her a sidelong glance. They sat next to each other on the carpeted hallway floor, both of them with their backs against the door. "Do you know what she said to me? She needed an adventure. The two of you have that in common I guess."

Tessa bit down on her lower lip and stared straight ahead. "Are you comparing me to your ex-wife?"

"No. I don't think if you were a mother that you'd let anything stand in the way of taking care of your child. I want to believe that about Delilah as well. I know it hasn't been easy, especially since I wasn't around much. My ex doesn't have a big family support network. I made some mistakes. I'm trying to make them right."

"You will," Tessa said. She straightened and then rose from the floor. "You'll figure it out."

He looked up. There were so many things he wanted to say, but he didn't know where to start. Mostly he wanted to pull her back down and wrap his arms around her. He wanted to take comfort in the feel of her and the way she made his heart peaceful.

He didn't reach for her, though. Tessa might not be like his ex-wife, but she had things to figure out. He understood her better now, especially after what she'd revealed tonight. Maybe she wasn't the bad-girl influence he'd first believed, but he also wasn't sure she was someone who could stick. Right now that's what he needed more than anything.

"Thank you for dinner," she said quietly.

"I'm sorry we got interrupted. I had big plans for you."

The smile she gave him was so sad it practically made his heart ache in response. "I might not have a lot of answers." She drew in a breath then blew it out like it cost her to release it. "But I know that nothing is certain in life, even the most carefully made plans. I'll see you and Lauren in the morning. Have a good night's sleep, Carson."

"You, too," he answered, but she was already walking away.

* * *

"So how did you leave it?"

Tessa placed her fork full of chicken saltimbocca back onto the plate and thought about how to answer Ella's question. "We left it with a lot of unspoken tension and unanswered questions. At this point, I don't know what to do next."

"Tell him you'll find a way to span whatever distance is between you," Cory suggested as she tied a bow around a bud vase. "A grand romantic gesture. That's exactly what you need."

Madison, who was standing behind Cory at the island in the Trophy Room kitchen, gave the bride-to-be a playful shove. "You want everyone on the love train because you've got stars in your eyes."

"I want my friend to be happy," Cory countered. "I think Carson Campbell makes her happy."

"She doesn't look happy at the moment." Madison pointed a finger at Tessa. "And you haven't even taken a bite of the chicken. It's not a real cooking club meeting if you don't eat."

"I'm not hungry, but I chopped onions," Tessa said in her own defense. "That counts." Ella, Cory and Madison stared at her. "What? It counts."

"Be honest, sweetheart." Cory reached across the island and patted Tessa's hand. "Did you chop those onions so you'd have an excuse to cry?"

"No. Not totally for that reason," she amended. "I

don't even have a reason to cry. Carson and I don't have an actual relationship. He's a friend with benefits. Those are a dime a dozen."

Madison shook her head. "I'm not disagreeing with you, and I've had way more experience in the casual sex department."

"You don't know that. I've had plenty of experience," Tessa lied. She didn't know why she insisted on keeping up the ruse. It was clear none of her friends were buying it. "I don't get it. I dress the part and act the part and talk the part. Why doesn't anybody believe that I'm a rebel?"

Ella's smile was uncharacteristically gentle. "It doesn't matter what we believe. The bigger question is why can't you believe that people can like you just the way you are?"

Tessa dashed a hand across her cheek. "Those stupid onions are still bothering me," she muttered.

"We know," her friends agreed. "It's all about the onions."

"You should at least talk to Carson," Cory suggested. "Yes, I want people to be happy, and I do have stars in my eyes because I'm getting married."

"Tomorrow," Tessa reminded her with a smile.

"Yeah," Cory agreed, "he's pretty awesome." Her gaze wandered to the door of the kitchen.

Jordan had closed down the restaurant tonight so that she could have her bachelorette party there.

When she'd assured him that her friends only wanted access to the kitchen, he'd invited a few of his buddies for a casual bachelors' evening in the main part of the bar. For all Tessa knew, Carson was out there with the guys right now. Somehow she doubted it, though. She couldn't imagine after those couple of days in Seattle that he'd be willing to let his daughter out of his sight.

She hoped she would see them at the wedding. "I didn't expect to like him the way I do," she said after a moment. "It was easier when I just thought he was a hot jerk."

Ella nodded. "The nice guys are the ones you have to watch out for. They are sneaky."

"Is there a nice guy you were thinking of in particular?" Tessa asked, happy to take the attention off herself for a moment.

"Nope." Ella took a big bite of chicken. "Although I did have a date last weekend with an accountant from Tacoma. I impressed him with my sausage ravioli. I never thought I'd find the day when I impressed a man with my cooking."

"Why don't you look happy about it?" Madison inclined her head. "Was he a vegetarian?"

Ella laughed. "No. Turns out he wasn't a nice guy. I wasted a decent meal on him."

"That's a bummer," Madison agreed. "That ravioli is amazing."

"I think I'm going to join my sister on the book tour," Tessa announced to her friends. "I need some time away."

The three of them looked equally horrified. "But you're going to come back, right?" Cory asked softly.

She shrugged. "Probably. But I'm not sure Starlight was ever supposed to be long-term for me. I just needed to prove to myself and to my family that I could make it on my own. I've done that now so…"

"This is your home, honey," Cory told her. Then she looked at Ella. "I know you've talked about leaving, too, but I don't want to hear that from either of you. You guys belong here. And Ben needs his aunties."

"I can be a long-distance auntie," Tessa offered.

"No." Madison said the word definitively. So much so that they all stopped then turned to her. She moved to the sink, aggressively loading plates into the dishwasher. "I like this place and I like you all in it, so there's no question. You two have to stay."

Tessa almost laughed at the absurdity of the declaration, but she could see that Madison was genuinely upset at the thought of their little friend posse breaking up. She didn't want that either.

"Okay, no more sad talking," Tessa told them. "This is a bachelorette party. It's supposed to be happy. Do you have any anatomically questionable pasta in the pantry?"

Madison laughed while Cory made a face.

"Then we'll do the next best thing," Cory said. She grabbed her laptop from her backpack. "Let's watch a falling-in-love movie montage on YouTube. It will get us in the mood for tomorrow."

"Perfect idea," Ella agreed. "Although nobody is going to be happier than Jordan when he sees you coming down the aisle."

"I love you guys." Corey dabbed at the corners of her eyes. "I wouldn't have gotten here without you."

"It doesn't matter where we all end up," Tessa promised her, "we'll be the best of friends. No matter what."

"No matter what," Madison and Ella agreed in unison.

"But you all have to stay," Cory added with a laugh. "Now gather round and let's watch some people fall in love."

Chapter Fifteen

"Daddy, I thought we were going to ride with Tessa?" Lauren pouted as she shouted out the question.

"We've already discussed this, Laur. Are you ready for me to curl your hair?" Carson poked his head out into the hallway when his daughter didn't answer. "I've watched a dozen videos and burned my fingertips so much that I have no feeling left. I think I should be great at it by now."

He started toward her bedroom when she didn't answer. He knew she was angry with him because she'd wanted to get ready with Tessa. Carson explained that since Tessa was part of the bridal party, she would have to go down to town early to be with the bride.

He walked into his daughter's bedroom to find her sitting on the bed, arms crossed as she glared at the floor in front of her. "You're not dressed," he pointed out.

"Tessa would have let me go with her," Lauren said. "I don't care that you're mad at her. She's still my friend."

"I'm not mad at Tessa."

"Then why don't you like her anymore?"

"I do like her." In fact he liked her way too much, which was a problem he didn't think Lauren would appreciate or understand.

"Then why couldn't I go with her?"

He crouched down in front of his daughter. "Because I want the prettiest girl in the world to be my date," he told her. "I know I'm not as good at doing hair and picking out clothes as your mom or Tessa, but I've missed a lot of your life, baby girl. I'm going to do my best to not miss any other moments."

"I don't want to move to Nashville," she said, her voice barely above a whisper. "I like it here."

Carson's heart felt like it might crack open. "I like it here, too. But more than anything, I want to be where you are. We'll talk to your mom and see if we can work something out, but just know that wherever you are is where I want to be."

She still didn't smile, but her features gentled. "Did you really burn the tips of your fingers on the curling iron?"

He held up his hands to show her. "Almost every single one."

"You'll get better with practice," she assured him and reached out to pat his shoulder. "Maybe not as good as the girls, but you'll get better."

"I'm trying." He held his breath as she stood, hoping it would be enough.

"I'm glad to be your date, Daddy." He breathed out, and his lungs felt like a weight was lifted off them. His daughter truly had him wrapped around her finger. He wouldn't have it any other way.

"Let's work on those curls," he said. She took his hand as she hopped off the bed. He wasn't actually as terrible at doing her hair as he thought he would be. Even Lauren was satisfied with his efforts, and that's all that counted.

By the time they were sitting in the small chapel where the wedding would take place, she was grinning at him. He'd do anything to keep her smiling. She turned, along with the rest of the guests, as the processional music started. Lauren waved to Tessa, who was walking down the aisle along with her friends.

She wore a navy blue cocktail dress with a slim silhouette that hugged her soft curves and was even more beautiful than Carson remembered. It had only been a couple of days since he'd seen her, but his heart ached like a lifetime had passed between them.

They watched as Cory followed her friends down the aisle, the white lace train of her gown flowing behind her.

"So pretty," Lauren whispered. The bride indeed looked beautiful, and more importantly, happy.

Carson glanced forward. Jordan stared at Cory like he had just lost his heart all over again. She stopped on her way down the aisle and kissed her baby, who was being held by a woman Carson had been introduced to as Jordan's mother. Carson envied their little family and the happiness that radiated from them.

He and Delilah had never found that level of happiness, but at that point in his life, he hadn't known enough about love to realize it was an option. His parents' marriage had been okay, but in some ways, more of a business arrangement than anything else. His mom had made being a military wife look easy. She'd done her duty, but he couldn't remember there being much true affection between his parents.

Growing up, that's what he thought was normal. So when he'd gotten married he hadn't given anything more to his wife. Their relationship had started hot and heavy. Delilah thrived on drama.

She liked arguing almost as much as she liked the

making up that came after and they'd gotten into a bad habit of fighting and then making their peace in the bedroom. When Carson's career ramped up, he'd grown tired of the drama. He had enough of that at work and just wanted a soft place to land when he came home. Delilah still wanted excitement and adventure. He hadn't been able or willing to give that to her.

As Cory and Jordan spoke their vows, Carson's gaze strayed to Tessa. She was watching them with a wistful look in her eyes and dabbing at the corners every few seconds.

How could he have thought she was anything like his ex-wife?

It didn't matter that she was sweet and steady. In her heart, she still wanted the same adventure and excitement Delilah had craved. Carson was even less able to get that now.

As if she could feel him watching her, she looked at him over the heads of the other wedding guests. For a moment, her gaze heated, and she flashed a small, private smile. Then he realized that none of their differences had to be an issue at the moment. They were going in two different directions, but for now, they were both here. He wanted her with a yearning that should have scared him. Hell, it did scare him. But he wanted her anyway and was tired of letting fears stand in the way.

* * *

"I should have guessed you'd be a crier at weddings."

Tessa's heart felt like it might beat right out of her chest as she turned to Carson, who stood just behind her.

He held out a glass of champagne, which she took and promptly drained. She didn't normally drink but her emotions had been all over the place today. There had been something powerful about hearing the vows Jordan and Cory spoke to each other, especially knowing the challenges they'd faced to get to that point.

All of that emotion had also made Tessa reflect on her life and imagining what it would be like to find that sort of love for herself. Plus, she'd received a call from the doctor that morning, calling to tell her the additional tests had come back normal. With everything going on inside her, she was surprised she hadn't gone through an entire box of tissues.

"Lots of people cry at weddings. They're happy tears."

He lifted a hand as if he might reach for her, then lowered it back to his side again. "That didn't come out right, which happens a lot when I'm talking to you. It wasn't a criticism. It's sweet, Tessa. You are sweet."

She rolled her eyes. "Sweet is for little girls and cotton candy."

"I'm sorry I pulled away after the scene with Delilah and her friends. That was stupid and wrong and didn't help anything. Mainly it irritated my daughter, who misses you like crazy."

"It's okay," she agreed, forcing herself to focus on the fact that he'd apologized and trying not to blurt out that she missed him and Lauren just as much. "Not a big deal. Honestly, I wondered if you'd show up today."

Nice, she inwardly congratulated herself. That sounded aloof and unfazed, just like she wanted to be.

"Lauren wouldn't have missed this for anything, and I wanted to see you."

"I live down the road from you. You could see me at any time."

"I wasn't sure you'd give me another chance."

"I shouldn't."

"You're right, but will you?" He bent his knees so they were at eye level. "Will you let me back in your life?"

"Friends with benefits?" she asked, needing to remind both of them of the parameters of their relationship.

Carson shook his head. "Friends. More than friends. Lauren and I both miss you, Tessa. I'm really sorry."

She could hear in his voice that he meant it, and

she did her best to harden her heart even as she felt her defenses melting once again. It was easier that way. Safer to push him out than to let him in. But wasn't that part of being brave? Facing the stuff that scared her. Her feelings for Carson terrified her.

Lauren ran up to the two of them at that moment. "Tessa, you look so pretty."

Tessa bent and hugged the girl. "Not nearly as pretty as you, sweetheart. You are a vision."

"Like a real princess."

"Even better," Tessa agreed.

"Daddy did my hair," Lauren told her. She turned her head so Tessa could admire her curls.

"He did a great job. You've got a fantastic daddy."

Lauren smiled at Carson almost shyly. "Yeah, he's pretty great." One of the other kids attending the reception called her name. "I've gotta go 'cause me and my friends are gonna dance. This is so much fun."

She skipped away to join a group of kids at the far end of the reception hall. "Who knew the way to a kid's heart was through a curling iron and ribbons?" Carson asked, massaging a hand over the back of his neck.

"You did good, Dad." Tessa smiled.

"But not with you."

"I'm not important."

He took her hand as the music changed to a ballad. "You're important to me. I'm sorry that I made you feel differently. Dance with me?"

Tessa glanced over his shoulder to see both Ella and Madison giving her an enthusiastic thumbs-up.

When she laughed softly, Carson turned then shifted his attention back to her. "Is it weird that I feel a huge sense of accomplishment that they were giving a thumbs-up instead of another kind of gesture?"

"It's a big deal," she confirmed then squeezed his fingers. "I'd like to dance with you."

Awareness tingled along her skin as he led her to the dance floor. The reception was being held in a converted barn on the outskirts of town. Under the twinkling lights that made up a canopy overhead, Tessa felt a bit like a princess herself.

"So have you really forgiven me?" he asked as he placed a hand on her waist.

Tessa smiled. "There's nothing to forgive. I don't hold grudges. That's one thing I learned from a lifetime of being sick. Cherish all of the moments you have and don't let what came before dictate the present. I'm not going to let the past control my future. I've done that for far too long."

"Am I part of your future, Tessa?"

She wanted to answer an unequivocal yes. That's how her heart felt. But she didn't trust it quite yet. Not with all of the uncertainty between them. "For now," she said, feeling like that was the best she could offer.

A sliver of her heart hoped Carson would argue, tell her he wanted to find a way to make it work for real between them. Not just neighbors who got together when they were lonely or needed some extra attention. She wanted to be more to him but didn't know how to ask for that. She was still learning how to be more to herself.

As if he could sense the discontent within her, Carson pulled her closer. More than anything, being closer to him was what she wanted. She snuggled in and held on as they swayed on the dance floor.

She might have more questions than answers in her life at the moment, but this felt right. It felt right to be with him. Wasn't part of adventure and being brave taking chances?

Would it be so strange if she and Carson found a way to take a chance on each other?

"You're going to need to fight," Josh said from where he sat across a table from Carson at Trophy Room three days after the wedding. As amazing as that night—and making up with Tessa—had been, things had gone to hell once again for him just as quickly. "Do you have an attorney? Because my brother is the best there is, and I'm sure he'd be happy to help you."

"We managed to get through a divorce and ten years of living separately without bringing attorneys into it." Carson gave a sharp shake of his head. "I don't want attorneys involved."

He'd called Josh and asked him to meet for a beer while Lauren was at a birthday party. He wasn't used to sharing his issues with anyone but figured his daughter was worth putting himself out there. Delilah had texted saying she would be back in the States along with Robbie in two weeks, right after school finished for the year. She wanted Carson to put Lauren on a plane to Chicago so she could be with her mother while the band did a three-day stint at Wrigley Field then played additional venues around the region.

In some ways, it would make Carson's life a lot easier. It would be a period of time he wouldn't have to deal with summer camps or balancing his work schedule with summer break. But after what had happened in Seattle, he didn't see how he could trust his ex-wife.

"It doesn't sound like she's giving you a choice," Josh said. "It's easy to not have attorneys involved or any formal custody agreement when you let her make all the rules. If that's changing then everything needs to change."

"It's going to make her mad," Carson said. "When Delilah is mad, she's not easy to deal with."

"Trust me, I get that. It's not fun to deal with period, but I don't see how you have a choice."

"I can avoid it by not antagonizing her."

"So you go to Nashville?" Josh asked. "What happens when she gets tired of that? You move to the next city or rent an RV so you can follow the tour bus around? That doesn't seem like a great life for you or Lauren."

Carson agreed, but he wasn't sure his opinion mattered.

"Not everybody can make single parenting look as easy as you do," he told his bearded friend.

"Don't you ever worry that your ex is going to come back and muck everything up?" he asked.

"Sometimes," Josh answered. "Other times, I want her to come back and see how amazing Anna is and what a mistake she made walking away from both of us."

Yes, their situations were different. Josh had ended up a single parent after his wife divorced him and cut off ties with their daughter when Anna was diagnosed with cancer in kindergarten.

Carson had heard the story from Tanya at the bar. The spunky bartender had apparently babysat most of the men in town and still felt very protective over a number of them, Josh included.

Anna was a plucky, gregarious and adorable kid. She'd been one of the girls that had made Lauren feel immediately welcome and her dad was much the same way. Truly Carson couldn't understand what Josh's ex-wife had been thinking.

"I don't want to put Delilah in that category. I know she loves Lauren, and she wants to be a part of her life. I didn't realize the toll that being a single mom was taking on her. That's on me and I want to make it right. But more than I want to make things right with her, I want to keep things right for Lauren."

Josh nodded. "I get that. But I can tell you without a doubt that twisting yourself up in knots to try to meet every one of your ex-wife's whims is not what's best for your daughter. You said she likes it here?"

"She loves it here."

"Then fight for her to be able to stay. For you to be able to stay." Josh gave him an assessing look. "Because you seem pretty happy here, too. Especially when Tessa Reynolds is involved." He scrunched up his brows. "She's different than I expected when I first met her."

"Me, too," Carson said with a laugh. "I'm not sure she's any better for Lauren than my ex. She might not be the wild party girl she wanted people to believe but…"

"But what?"

"She wants excitement and adventure in her life.

I'm a single dad whose idea of a good time is managing to stay awake until ten."

"I can think of some fun things to do going to bed early if you're with the right person." Josh smiled. "Maybe Tessa can be your person."

"I think Tessa wants to concentrate on being her own person," Carson admitted. "Speaking of right people, what's the deal with you and Ella Samuelson?"

Josh's fingers tightened ever so slightly on the pint glass. "There's no deal."

"There's definitely a deal," Carson said. "I can't decide if the two of you look at each other more often like you want to rip each other's throats out or you want to rip the other person's clothes off."

"For sure the throat."

"You know what they say about a thin line between love and hate."

Josh snorted. "There's no line with Ella and me. She doesn't like me."

"And how do you feel about her?"

"How I feel is irrelevant based on how much she doesn't like me."

Josh popped the last jalapeño popper into his mouth and chewed. He pulled a wallet out of his backpack, drew a business card from it and handed it to Carson. "This is Parker's number. Give him a call. He can help you. Don't think about it as hurting your ex-wife or making her life difficult. You're making your daughter's life better, and she's the priority."

Carson nodded as he took the thick white business card and put it into his back pocket. "I'll consider talking to him," he said. "You're right about Lauren being my priority. She's what matters most, and I'm going to do everything in my power to protect her."

Chapter Sixteen

Tessa was behind the bar at the Thirsty Chicken when she heard the familiar high-pitched voice.

She turned and scanned the crowd because it was impossible that Lauren Campbell would be at the bar on a busy night like this one. She'd seen Lauren and Carson just last night for dinner at their house. Since the wedding, she'd spent several evenings with Carson. By tacit agreement, they didn't discuss the future or expectations. It was as if they both knew their time together was limited and they were going to enjoy it.

He was now working toward a custody agreement with Delilah while Tessa's sister was giving even more pressure to Tessa about joining her on the book tour. A big piece of Tessa didn't want to leave Starlight, but she also wanted the adventure that touring with Julia could provide. Again, she'd decided not to decide. Not yet.

"Hey, Tessa."

She gave herself a mental headshake and focused on Travis, one of the barbacks. "There's a kid by the pool tables asking for you."

Her heart seemed to stutter to a stop. "A kid? A girl?"

"Yeah. Blond hair. Real cute."

Tessa could barely breathe as she rushed toward the back of the bar, unable to fathom why Lauren would be there. She spotted the girl's honey-colored hair and moved forward, only to come up short as the woman sitting across from Lauren rose and gave her a steely glare.

"You must be my daughter's new friend."

"Hi, Tessa," Lauren said, turning in her chair. "Mommy came to pick me up from school and we were trying to figure out a place to go and get dinner. I told her about you working here, and so we came."

"Well, I'm always glad to see you." Tessa was happy her voice didn't shake as she turned to Carson's ex-wife. "It's nice to meet you, Delilah."

The woman gave a throaty laugh. "Nice," she repeated. "Right." She dug in her pocket and pulled out a handful of coins. "Hey, honey, will you go play on the pinball machine while Tessa and I have grown-up talk for a minute, okay?"

"Mom," Lauren ground out. "I hate pinball and grown-up talk."

"Lauren Nicole." Tessa understood Delilah's purposeful use of her daughter's full name.

Clearly, Lauren did as well. "Fine. Tessa, could I get a root beer?"

"Sure, sweetie. Let me just talk to your mom for a minute and I'll get one for you." The back of the bar wasn't crowded yet, so Tessa didn't worry about Lauren walking a few feet away to deposit coins into the vintage pinball machine. She wouldn't let anything happen, and she knew the bouncer would be watching out for the girl as well.

She pursed her lips as she shifted her attention back toward Delilah. "Why do you have her here? She shouldn't be here. Does Carson know?"

"You don't have to worry about my ex-husband or my daughter," Delilah said, her voice silky smooth.

"I will worry," Tessa countered. "I care about them both. Maybe you should start worrying, too."

She quickly shut her mouth. This was not her fight, and she had no right to insert herself into it. Yes, Carson and Lauren meant something to her. She cared about them. She loved them.

The thought had her sucking in a quick breath of air. It didn't come as a shock. She'd known she was falling in love with the single dad and his adorable daughter. She just hadn't allowed herself to admit it because it felt too scary to risk herself that way. Not when his life was so uncertain and when she still had questions looming about her health.

She could never expect him to commit to her or take on one more responsibility when there was no guarantee she would stay healthy. It had been bad enough being a burden on her family. She certainly wouldn't allow herself to be a burden to him.

"I know you love your daughter," she said, not wanting to antagonize Carson's ex. Tessa wanted to defuse this situation and get Lauren back to Starlight and under the protection of her father.

"You aren't his type." Delilah gave Tessa a critical once-over. "He likes a woman with experience who knows her way around the world. You might think working in a place like this means something. That it makes you tough."

She poked a finger into Tessa's shoulder. "It's obvious to me, and probably to everyone else here, that you are like a baby bird who can't even leave the nest to fly. Carson isn't going to take care of you, little bird."

"I'm not asking him to." Tessa rubbed her shoulder.

"Of course you are. I know your type, and I know his type. He is a sucker for a lost soul. You fit that mold, but I have plans for my life and my daughter."

"Did you really consider your daughter when you made those plans?" Tessa couldn't help but ask. It was one thing to knock on her, but she wasn't going to stand here and let this woman pretend to be mother of the year when she knew that wasn't the case.

"I know about you, Tessa Reynolds." Delilah's kohl-rimmed eyes narrowed. "It doesn't take much to pull up your pathetic history on the internet. Always the poor little sick girl."

Tessa's stomach burned at the accusation, especially because she hated that part of herself and that she'd been too weak to fight it until recently. "My life is none of your business."

Carson's ex-wife gave an angry snort of laughter. "If you are inserting yourself into my daughter's life then you are my business. And don't pretend to be shy about it. From everything I can tell, your sister has built a career off of your story."

"My sister has helped a lot of people."

"You top that list, right? Her assistant." Delilah made exaggerated air quotes with her fingers. "Relying on family to give you a job. Your life has been a cakewalk, sis."

Tessa felt like she'd been slapped. "You have no right to say that to me." She forced a smile when

Lauren looked back over her shoulder. "You don't know me."

"I'm not sure what you think is going to happen between you and Carson, but leave him alone. If he wants to be a part of Lauren's life, it will be on my terms. He can come to Nashville or he can go back to being a birthday and Christmas parent. But I'm not going to have him distracted by some little bird who wants an instant family. Go make your own."

As much as the words hurt, Tessa tried to remember what was most important right now: Lauren and Carson. She didn't know why her presence in their lives triggered Delilah so badly, but that wasn't her concern.

"Carson can make his own decisions as a grown man. He may not have been as involved when Lauren was younger, but he's doing the right thing now. He wants to do that for her. He knows she's with you, right?"

Something like guilt flashed across Delilah's features. "I'm her mother. I don't need permission to pick up my daughter from school or take her for the day. I'm her mother," she repeated as she stood from the table, sounding on edge in a way Tessa didn't like.

"Yes, you have the right." Tessa rose as well when Delilah took a step closer to her. "But Carson needs to know where Lauren is. He's going to be scared to death otherwise."

"It's not your business. Let me deal with Carson and my daughter." Delilah gave Tessa a little shove. "You stay out of our lives."

"Keep your hands off of me," Tessa said. She might not have a lot of experience with standing up for herself, but she certainly wasn't going to let this woman push her around. She let her disease and fear and her parents control her. Those days were over. She also wasn't dumb enough to get in a fight with Delilah.

She straightened her shoulders and did her best to look strong and intimidating. Or at least like someone who couldn't be pushed around. "I'm calling Carson now. What you're doing isn't right."

She pulled her phone out of the back pocket of her miniskirt only to have Delilah slap it away. "Stay in your lane, Redbird."

Heart pounding and palms clammy, Tessa reached for her phone. Delilah shoved her hip into Tessa's shoulder, making her stumble back a step. "Stop that," she said on a hiss of breath.

They'd started drawing attention from clusters of nearby patrons. One of the regulars, a middle-aged mom with a hardscrabble past with whom Tessa had become friends, gave her a questioning look. Tessa shook her head. She didn't want to cause a scene.

"I'll call Carson when I want him to know where I am." Delilah leaned forward as Tessa regained her footing. "I'm her mother."

"No one is denying that," Tessa said, then couldn't help but add when her mounting frustration got the best of her, "You sure aren't acting like a good one right now."

The punch caught her by surprise and knocked her onto her backside.

"Oh, hell, no," she heard one of the patrons mutter while a male voice yelled out, "Girl fight."

Then all hell broke loose.

Carson sat on the sofa in his darkened living room later that night, staring at the front door to his house. He glanced at the clock on the wall. Ten after midnight.

Only one person would be knocking at this hour, and he was still so angry he wasn't sure he could see her without lashing out.

He'd been frantic with worry in the hours after the school administrator explained that Lauren had been checked out of class by her mother before the last bell.

He'd called Delilah repeatedly, but it had gone to voice mail every time, and she hadn't responded to any of his text messages. Things had gotten so desperate, he'd tried to track down her rock-star boyfriend in Madrid, where his band was headlining a spring music festival.

It was a terrifying feeling to be so out of control. One of the other mothers, Brynn Dunlap, had witnessed his heated conversation with the elementary school principal and immediately called her husband, Nick, who happened to be the town's sheriff.

Carson had met both of them at Jordan and Cory's wedding. They seemed like a nice couple, although as a rule, he didn't want to be in a position to need the services of local law enforcement.

But he was beside himself with worry. The hours before the police chief in Montrose had called to say his daughter was at their local station had been the longest of his life.

After a quick call with Lauren to assure himself that she was okay and some convoluted story she'd told between sobs about Delilah and Tessa getting in a fight, he'd raced toward his truck to make the thirty-minute drive. Nick had stopped him with an offer of an escort, and he'd followed the sheriff, sirens and lights blazing to the nearby town.

Luckily, Nick had already called that station so Delilah wasn't able to whisk his daughter away again.

They'd had a huge fight in the station's lobby, which had sent Lauren into another fit of crying.

Carson had forced himself to reclaim a calm demeanor so he wouldn't upset Lauren any more than she already was. Delilah sported a bloody lip and a nasty scrape above one eye and was railing about the low-life women who hung out at the Thirsty Chicken.

"What the hell were you doing there in the first place?" he'd demanded of his ex-wife.

She'd shrugged in response. "Lauren couldn't stop talking about your little chippy, so I wanted to check her out."

Tessa.

"And you two got in a fistfight?"

"She and her friends started it," Delilah had insisted.

And while Carson found that hard to believe, he didn't have any way to refute her story. Everyone involved in the altercation from the bar had left the police station by the time he'd arrived, even Tessa.

She'd gotten in a fight with his ex-wife then left his daughter behind.

After another round of persistent knocking, he finally opened the door, telling himself that it was better to have this conversation while Lauren was asleep. No doubt his daughter would not appreciate the decision Carson felt he had to make.

But his heart jumped in his chest when he saw Tessa standing on the other side with her messy hair, smudged makeup and giant shiner.

His first inclination—swift and sure—was to pull her into his arms and make sure she was okay. Almost as quickly, he forced himself to reject that as a possibility.

He shored up his defenses and cocked an eyebrow. "What do you want?"

"How's Lauren?" she asked quietly.

"Finally asleep and I hope she wakes up with very little memory of this horrible night."

"Me, too."

"I don't want you near her, Tessa."

"You can't mean that. Carson, please…" She bit down on her lower lip when her voice hitched, and he could see the effort it took for her to keep her composure.

He could see the pain in her expression, and it hurt his heart. But he also felt frantic and desperate. Even now with his daughter safely tucked into her bed, the terror of her going missing kept a hold on him. He couldn't release it, and Tessa was part of that.

The choices she'd made in her life had put Lauren at risk. His choice to care about Tessa had caused Lauren pain. The most important thing he was charged with accomplishing in his life was protecting his girl. The only thing that mattered was loving her and keeping her safe. He hadn't done that.

"Delilah said you and your friends started the fight."

"And you believed her?"

"You left the police station."

"Because I didn't want to upset Delilah even more than I had. I was thinking about Lauren."

He shook his head. "No. If you had been thinking about her, the situation never would have escalated. I understand that you want to put on this persona of the bad girl. A rebel who can do whatever she wants in life without consequences. Without considering the implications. But there are always consequences, Tessa."

Her bright blue eyes went dark. "You think I don't know about consequences and choices? Do you believe with everything you know about me and what's between us that I would risk your daughter's safety?"

"What's really between us?"

She took a step back like his words were a physical punch to the gut. Some small scrap of rational thought whispered that he was being unfair. He was lashing out at Tessa because she was an easy target. He had handled fatherhood badly for a decade and that's why he was in this position in the first place.

He could blame Tessa or Delilah for the circumstance all he wanted, but the truth was it fell on him and he didn't know how to fix it.

What Carson understood was how to fall back on his family background and training. Forward-thinking. Eliminate the weaknesses. Focus on his strengths. Right now, Tessa was a weakness.

She'd made him want things he knew were out of reach. Things like a real home and a real family.

What he wanted didn't matter. It wouldn't matter if he was in Starlight or Nashville or somewhere else if it would keep the peace with Delilah and ensure Lauren wasn't hurt in the process. He would upend his life over and over again. He'd made enough choices putting himself first. Now he had no choice but to do what was in his daughter's best interest.

"I love her, Carson." Tessa swept a hand across her cheek. "Just like I love you. Don't shut me out. I wanted to pretend to be a rebel and a bad girl or someone that wasn't truly me. You helped me see that accepting myself is the bravest thing that I can do. I'm good for your daughter, and I'm good for you. I believe that with my whole heart. We are good for each other. I don't know how tonight went so sideways but it wasn't my intention. I'm sorry I couldn't stop it. You have to know I would never put Lauren at risk. Not on purpose."

Carson couldn't understand why doing the right thing felt so wrong, but he held true to what he believed. If anything, the way his heart felt like it was breaking in half was a sign. A sign that being with Tessa was a distraction he couldn't afford anymore.

"Live your life, Tessa. Go with your sister or stay in Starlight. Your decisions don't matter to me. You don't matter to me."

He waited for her to call him out on the obvious lie. She had to be able to see how much this was killing him. Tears were streaming down her face, and she didn't even bother to wipe them away.

"You're a coward," she said, her voice barely above a whisper. "All your big talk about dedication and sticking it out. Then at the first challenge, you cut and run."

"I'm not running," he protested. "I'm standing up for my daughter."

"You're wrong. You're teaching her that when things get hard, it's easier to shut down than open up. I was ready to be brave for you, Carson. It's a shame you couldn't handle it. But I'm going to be better. I'm going to be okay on my own. You helped me see that. Maybe I owe you."

Oh, how this woman got to him. Even as he was breaking both of their hearts, her generous spirit shined through. Truly he didn't deserve her.

"I'll stay away from Lauren and you." All of the emotion had drained from her voice, and he hated himself for causing that. "You're also making the biggest mistake of your life. I might not have the experience some women do…" She straightened her shoulders and gave him a glare worthy of a queen. "But I'm worthy of being loved just the way I am. I know that for sure."

When she turned on her heel and disappeared into

the darkness, he wanted to go after her. But his feet remained rooted to the floor as his heart cracked into a hundred jagged pieces.

Chapter Seventeen

"You can't leave."

"I can't stay."

Tessa sat cross-legged on the cabin's overstuffed sofa two days later, her friends surrounding her. She hadn't called them at first after the breakup—or whatever it was—certainly a breaking of her heart. She'd felt sad and humiliated that she'd assumed she and Carson were something more than just neighbors with benefits.

Maybe her inexperience was to blame, but she didn't think that was it. She had truly fallen for Carson and not because she didn't know any better. He was solid and caring and made her feel like she could be something more. Someone worth loving.

His rejection didn't invalidate her feelings. It simply obliterated her heart.

"This is your home." Madison said the words so forcefully that Tessa startled.

"My temporary home," she clarified.

"Your home without qualification," Ella said.

Word traveled fast in a small town, and she'd received a flurry of texts from her friends earlier in the morning asking if she was okay. There was no question with any of them that she had been the wronged party in whatever happened with Carson's ex-wife. Her battered heart appreciated their loyalty.

It was one thing to buy new clothes and experiment with makeup. But she'd gone into town for coffee at Main Street Perk that morning and hadn't liked the sidelong glances she'd received from people she barely knew. Clearly people blamed her for the altercation with Delilah and the melee that ensued at the Thirsty Chicken. As if she were at fault for the mental anguish Carson had gone through when he thought his daughter was missing.

No one who knew her would ever believe that she'd put a child in danger or act irresponsibly when it came to a situation like the one she'd found herself in.

She thought Carson knew her. In truth, she hadn't

given much consideration to what all her posturing and pretending would mean for her in the town and how striving to be someone different from the person she was could backfire.

"How can this be my home when I haven't even been myself here?" she asked, more to herself than to her friends.

Cory reached across the table and squeezed her hand. It wasn't an official cooking club meeting but Madison had brought lobster mac and cheese and homemade bread, claiming they all needed a bit of comfort food to solve Tessa's issues.

Tessa didn't have an appetite for the scrumptious food Madison had prepared, but she appreciated the solidarity of the effort.

"We know who you are," Cory said.

Madison nodded. "Girl, we knew you were pretending all along. Plenty of people did."

"Not all of them. Not Carson."

"He knows you." This was from Ella, who pointed a fork full of mac and cheese in Tessa's direction. "He just forgot because that stupid ex of his got in his head. That doesn't mean you should cut and run. Let people know the real you."

"I'm not even sure if I know who that is. I'm not the sick girl. And I'm a colossal failure at being a bad girl."

All three of her friends laughed in response to that last statement.

Tessa frowned. "I mean I probably wasn't horrible."

"Horrible," Ella confirmed.

"The worst," Madison added.

"I have to agree," Cory admitted.

"I think going with my sister might be the break I need." Tessa said the words slowly like she was trying out the taste of them. "It will be a good chance for me to be me. To take the tour to figure out myself."

Madison let out a soft snort. "Good luck with that."

"What do you mean?"

"I've read your sister's book."

"Really?" Tessa looked surprised. "You don't seem like the personal development type."

Madison shrugged. "When I stopped drinking, I was the type who would try anything to stay on the wagon. Religion. Yoga. Self-help gurus. I wasn't picky."

"You're not a fan of Julia?"

"I have no problem with what your sister does. But her work is framed by your illness. Do you think you're going to be her sidekick for the summer and not fall back into a situation where your identity is the sick sister? The one who needs to be rescued?"

Tessa hated the truth of what Madison said, but she wasn't exactly doing a bang-up job on her own.

"I'm absolute trash at this reinvention thing. Maybe I could learn something from Dr. J."

Ella clucked disapprovingly. "You are not a failure." She pointed a finger at herself. "I'm a failure."

"Neither of you are failures." Cory straightened. "It offends me that you think so. You three are the best friends I've ever had. What does that say about me if I pick loser friends?"

Madison raised a hand. "I'm not a loser. I was a loser back when I was drinking and torpedoing my life. I've gotten smarter. Tessa, stop being stupid and get smarter."

Tessa barked out a laugh. "I take it the self-development track was short-lived because that doesn't sound like the kind of pearls of wisdom my sister dispenses." She thought about the conversation she'd had with Julia in Seattle and the advice her sister had offered about finding her path.

"You're running away," Ella insisted. "Since that was my plan, I find it offensive that you beat me to it."

"You have family here," Tessa pointed out, "and a great career."

"I'm temporarily answering phones at the bank my family owns. You think you're pathetic working for your sister. What does that make me?"

"But you have options. You're a nurse. You've

been all around the world for your work. It's not the same."

"It's not," Ella agreed, "because I couldn't handle it. I couldn't handle seeing kids who were sick or had few options in life. I didn't know how to deal with the hard stuff, so I came back here to stick my head in the sand and ignore it. You came here for a fresh start. You need to think about what you've learned, what you can do next and what you can do with all of those lessons. You aren't the sick girl. You aren't the rebel. You don't need a book tour getting coffee for your sister to figure out who you really are, Tessa. You need to stick it out."

Tessa swallowed against the emotion that bubbled up in her throat. "How can I stay in this town when Carson hates me? I told him I loved him and he said he doesn't want to see me again. He doesn't trust me with his daughter. You didn't see how people were looking at me in the coffee shop. He's not the only one who believes the worst about me."

"Then prove them wrong," Cory said.

Ella nodded. "Prove us right."

"I don't know if I have it in me." Tessa hated the truth in her words, but what else could she tell them? "No matter what I decide, I want you to know how much I appreciate each of you. I didn't know I could have friends like you guys."

"Oh, no." Madison shook her head. "If you're

going to get all sentimental then we need to find some onions and start chopping because I'm not crying without onions. I am not a crier."

Cory gave her a little nudge. "I saw you dabbing at the corners of your eyes at my wedding. You were totally crying."

Madison shoved back. "Pollen in my eyes."

Tessa laughed. It felt good and strange to laugh in the midst of her heartache, and she appreciated her friends for being the kind of people who could do that for her. "Will we still be friends if I leave?" she blurted.

"No," Madison said. "Not in any way."

"She's right." Ella plopped down into the chair next to Tessa. "I can only be friends with people who live within a twenty-mile radius of me."

Tessa's heart sank. She never dreamed that...

Suddenly Ella's arm wrapped around her shoulders. "Don't be such a goober. Of course we will be friends. Heck, we'll do virtual cooking clubs if we need to."

Tessa looked at Madison. "I was joking," the cool blonde said. "We'll still be friends."

"Definitely still friends, no matter what," Cory echoed. "But we still want you to stay."

"I love you guys." Tessa hadn't been sure she'd ever say those words out loud again after the way

Carson had responded to them, but her friends gathered around her for some awkward hugging.

If nothing else, her time in Starlight had given her these women, and she would forever be grateful for them...no matter where life took her next.

In the end, Tessa decided to do both. She would stay in Starlight but join Julia for different stops on the tour. Maybe she wasn't being as strong as she should, but maybe part of strength was admitting that she needed a bit of a break.

In truth, she also wanted to prove to herself and her sister that she wasn't the sick girl who had first inspired Julia in her work. She was strong and healthy, a partner in her sister's career success. She wanted a chance to hold her head up and be seen as someone different. Not a pretend person who she'd made up like a fictional character or a costume she tried on. She wanted to be true to herself.

She had also talked to her aunt and told her that she would be renting a place on her own closer to downtown once the tour ended and she was back in Starlight full-time. Strength was one thing, but driving by Carson's house every day would be like stabbing herself in the heart.

It had only taken an hour to pack up the makeup and clothes that had never truly fit her into boxes to pitch and donate. This was her new life, the one she had chosen, and she would make it work without him but that didn't ease the ache inside her.

She was packing the afternoon before she was scheduled to fly to New York City where the tour would begin. They'd be traveling along the Eastern Seaboard and then to Nashville and Atlanta before she'd returned to Starlight to pack up the rest of her things and move.

She had to believe that the distance would help heal her heart. Although the past couple of nights had been harder than she could have imagined. And the days. Yesterday afternoon, she'd seen the soccer teams practicing on the field as she'd driven through downtown. Carson and Lauren had both been easy to spot, and Tessa knew there would be a hole in her heart going forward without the two of them in her life.

There was a shout from the front of the house, followed by someone frantically knocking at the front door. She flung it open to see a distraught Lauren standing on the other side.

"He's gone, Tessa," she screamed. "They have to find him. We have to help them find him."

Tessa glanced behind the nearly hysterical girl to see her teenage babysitter standing at the edge of the porch looking absolutely stricken.

"She overheard me," the girl said, her lips barely moving. "I wasn't supposed to tell her."

"Tell her what?" She crouched down and put her arms around Lauren. "What happened, sweetheart?" Lauren just cried into her chest. Tessa looked at the babysitter again and repeated the question. "What happened?"

The girl rolled her lips together. "I wasn't supposed to—"

"It's too late for that. Tell me." Tessa's heart hammered in her chest.

"Her dad was scheduled to fly back from Portland and land about an hour ago. He hasn't returned and they haven't been able to make contact with the plane." The teenager wrapped her arms tight around herself. "There's some weather between here and Oregon and they aren't sure—"

"Enough." Lauren had started to cry harder. Tessa peeled the girl away and held her at arm's length. "Look at me," she commanded. "Your daddy is an amazing pilot. He would never risk a flight if he thought it was unsafe. He's going to be okay. He's going to come home."

"Do you promise?" Lauren drew in a shaky breath. "How do you know, Tessa?"

Tessa didn't know and she couldn't promise, but she believed it with her whole being.

"I know because I feel it here." She pressed a hand to her chest and drew Lauren forward again.

"You feel it, too, don't you? He's going to come back safely."

The babysitter made a face. "I don't think you—"

"Go on home," Tessa told the girl. "Lauren can stay with me. I'll take her back to her house after a while. We'll wait for word about her father there."

She shouldn't make the offer. After all, Carson had been quite clear that he didn't want her anywhere near his daughter. But there was no way Tessa would leave the little girl alone at this time.

The teen looked relieved. "Okay," she agreed. "Let me know when you hear what happens with… you know."

"Yes, I will."

"I'll see you later, Lauren," the girl called out weakly. Lauren didn't look at her.

"She thinks he crashed," the girl whispered to Tessa. "She thinks he's not coming back."

"You don't have to worry about what anyone thinks," Tessa promised Lauren, refusing to allow any doubt to creep into her mind or tone. "Nothing is going to stop your father from coming back to you."

She brought Lauren inside her cabin and settled her in front of the TV. Then she called the sheriff's office and asked to talk to Nick Dunlap. She explained that Lauren was with her and would remain there until Carson made it home.

Nick's tone didn't give much away, but Tessa was

an expert at picking up on subtle cues. She'd had a lot of experience in her life measuring the way people reacted to her, especially when she was at her sickest. His clipped syllables told her everything she needed to know about the severity of the situation. He had very few details about what was going on but helped her piece together a little bit more of the circumstances.

The situation didn't seem hopeful. But Tessa wouldn't contemplate anything but a positive outcome. Not when Lauren's heart was at stake. She called Madison next and asked the chef to bring food up the mountain.

Less than thirty minutes later, her friend arrived at Carson's cabin. Tessa had walked Lauren down to her own home, figuring she'd be more comfortable waiting there. Madison also brought her black Lab, Gracie, and the dog was exactly the distraction Lauren needed. She took the animal into the front yard to throw a ball and it gave her something to focus on other than where her dad might be.

Madison stayed with them until Tessa finally sent her away long after dark had fallen. There had been no update on Carson. She knew that the more time that went by, the more dire the potential outcome. She hated not knowing and wished she could drive out into the wilderness to search for him herself. She wanted to do something useful but also understood that a scared little girl needed her. It didn't matter what had come between her and Carson or how they'd each let fear ruin the potential of their future.

Lauren was the most important thing at the moment.

Hours ticked by, and they watched old movies and ate a bit of the lasagna Madison had brought. Neither one of them had much of an appetite, and after a while, she simply sat on the couch under a blanket with Lauren snuggled up next to her.

She wouldn't have thought she could fall asleep with so much fear and worry pounding through her, but she must've dozed off because the next thing she knew a gentle hand was smoothing the hair back from her face. She looked up and gasped as Carson stared down at her.

"It's you," she whispered, feeling an equal mix of relief and embarrassment at her stupid reaction. Tears filled her eyes, and she quickly blinked them away.

"I'm okay," he said just as quietly. "The plane went down in a remote location so I had no service and it took hours to hike out. Other than a few scratches I'm fine."

She swallowed and nodded, unable to put together a coherent sentence.

"You stayed with her." He glanced between Tessa and his daughter. She wished she could read the emotion in his eyes, but she was too busy trying to hold herself together.

"Yes. I'm sorry if that upsets you. I know you don't want me in her life, but she needed somebody she felt comfortable with today."

He shook his head and squeezed shut his eyes for a long moment. "Tessa. I don't know—"

"Daddy." Lauren scrambled up off the sofa and launched herself into her father's arms as she tossed the blanket into Tessa's lap.

"I was so scared, Daddy. What happened? Are you all right? Did you crash the plane?"

Tessa rose as Carson explained the circumstances to his daughter and reassured her that he was fine.

She wanted to stay. She wanted to be part of this reunion. She wanted these two people to be her family. But they weren't. They didn't belong to her, and there was no point in pretending otherwise.

"Tessa."

She heard Carson say her name when she was almost to the door but didn't look back. She held up a hand and let herself out into the darkness, craving the empty night the way the child craved her favorite stuffed animal. As relieved as she felt that Carson had returned, her insides shouldn't feel like they were hollowed out from the emptiness of moving on without him. But she knew that the pain would be her companion for a long time to come.

Chapter Eighteen

It had been five days since Carson had landed his plane in the remote wilderness of the Cascade Mountains. He'd been in dangerous situations before. Hell, his career in the military had been all about risk and adrenaline.

But all he'd been able to think about when he was trying to get to safety were the two people he'd left behind. He would have done anything to return to his daughter. There was no doubt he had plenty of reasons to judge himself for how much of her life he'd missed. He was also just as determined not to waste that time again.

During the harrowing landing in the dense forest with almost zero visibility, he'd only been able to think about surviving the crash. As he'd worked his way through the forest, he'd spent almost as much time reliving those last moments with Tessa. The pain on her face and knowing he'd caused it. The angry words he'd spoken out of fear. The way she'd been brave with her heart when he'd given her every reason to turn away from him.

And then to return and find the two of them together. It made his heart crack open in an entirely new way.

He'd been such a fool not to trust her. Yeah, she put up a million masks and walls to hide behind, but he should have known. His heart knew hers and he should have trusted her.

He wanted to tell her that and so much more, but she'd left before he could.

He still didn't quite understand how she managed to be so generous with his daughter and loyal to him in the wake of how badly he'd behaved. There had been no mistaking what he'd seen in her eyes when she'd woken and gazed up at him.

Apparently, he'd hurt her so much it didn't matter. She was going to be smart enough not to give him another chance.

He'd tried. He'd gone to her cabin the next morning only to find it empty. It hadn't taken much digging in town to hear that she'd left to go on tour with her sister.

She'd left him behind.

He could only wish her well. Wasn't that what you were supposed to do for someone you loved? But his heart screamed in protest. His life felt empty without her.

Lauren had slipped back into her normal routine after the fear of losing him faded, although he knew she missed Tessa as much as he did. Carson had met with Josh's brother to go over his legal options for custody.

After the stunt Delilah pulled, he was no longer willing to go along with anything his ex-wife wanted or her whims as far as parenting. Lauren deserved better, and he was going to give it to her.

He had no idea how long it would take to patch up the hole left in both of their lives by Tessa's absence.

He was going to do his best. Kids were resilient, right? Certainly more so than him.

He hadn't slept since the night of the crash, at least that's what it felt like. Between coming down from the adrenaline rush of landing a plane with his life on the line to the upheaval with his ex, to losing Tessa, his mind refused to calm.

But he was still on the sidelines running the team's soccer practice. It was a perfect early summer evening with temperatures hovering in the mid-seventies and the scent of freshly cut grass carrying on the breeze.

Another mom had stepped up to be a coach alongside him, and he was learning to navigate the world of being a coach to a group of newbie athletes. To enjoy their pleasure in the game instead of worrying about anything else.

"Daddy, Miriam is going to get ice cream with her grandparents. Can I go with her and you can pick me up at the shop?"

His daughter's happiness eased some of the ache in his chest. He agreed to the plan and continued to collect cones and balls from the field.

"You're stupid." He froze at the accusation then turned slowly to find Madison, Cory and Ella staring at him.

"We were going to handle this diplomatically," Cory said with a wry look at the clearly angry chef.

"I didn't use any four-letter words," Madison countered. "That feels diplomatic to me."

"Good point," Cory agreed. She scrunched up her nose and gave Carson an angry look. "She's right. You're stupid."

"I was going to fix it," he said by way of defense. It sounded weak to his own ears. "I wanted to make it better. I went to her cabin but she had already left."

"Because you were so mean to her," Ella pointed out.

"She didn't leave because of me." He said the

words with more certainty than he felt. "She wanted to go on tour with her sister."

The three women stared at him so hard that Carson felt himself fidget like a little boy under the watchful glare of a strict teacher.

He shoved the final soccer ball into the mesh bag and tried to look casual. They continued to stare. "What?" he asked finally. "Just say it. It feels like you're trying to turn me to stone with those death looks."

"We are attempting to glare some sense into you," Ella explained.

Madison nodded. "Is it working?"

"What kind of sense? What do you expect me to do?"

Madison immediately began to answer, but Cory held up a hand. She stepped forward. "Before we clue you in, tell us one thing. Do you love Tessa?"

A denial almost escaped his lips because his personal life was no one's business. Why would he admit to being hopelessly in love with a woman who wanted nothing to do with him—even rightfully so after how he treated her.

Carson wasn't exactly comfortable with vulnerability and pushing down the difficult emotions had always been easier than dealing with them. But there was something about Tessa's friends seeking him out that gave him a glimmer of hope.

Not to mention the fact that she'd stayed with his daughter during Lauren's darkest hour.

Added to that was how much he missed her.

Even if she returned to Starlight and still wouldn't give him another chance, somehow he thought it would be easier. The sight of her gave him a feeling of peace and contentment he'd never had before and he wanted the opportunity to prove she could trust him with her heart. And she'd said that he'd helped her. He didn't want to throw away the connection between them if there was even the slightest chance of fixing things.

Her friends wouldn't be here if all hope was lost. Would they? Before he lost his nerve, he nodded. "I love her. I know I hurt her. I don't deserve her. I'm a complete idiot, just like you said. But, yes. I love her with my whole heart."

"Then you're not a *complete* idiot." Madison leaned forward and patted his arm, her dark eyes more amused than angry at this point. "Just mostly one."

How sad had his life become that Carson actually took comfort in that? "She wants a new start without me. It's clear because she left."

"Tessa is figuring things out," Cory said. "She left because she wants a new start with her sister." She glanced at the other two women. "She loves you even though you hurt her, although none of us know if she'll give you another chance."

"What we do know is you're not going to find out by sitting on your keister around here." This insight came from Ella.

He didn't disagree but… "If she's coming back…"

There went the disapproving stares again.

"Okay, I get it. I messed up really badly and now I need to fix it in a big way. Sooner than later."

"You do," Ella confirmed.

If only he had the first clue as to how to make that happen. His mind raced with the possibilities. There were plenty of excuses why he couldn't put himself out there until she got back. He had a job. He had Lauren to think about. Hell, Tessa would understand that. She'd been nothing but understanding about making his daughter the priority. Which only confirmed that he needed to try harder. He needed to give of himself the same way she had. Without question or reservation.

"I need help," he said quietly, breathing in the fresh spring air and feeling a bit of relief from the vise that seemed to have his heart in a stranglehold. "I don't even know where she is."

There was another beat of silent communication between the women, and then Cory smiled. "We can help you, Carson, but just know that it's your only shot. Because if you hurt our friend again, there won't be anything left of you to save."

"Fair enough," he agreed as hope bloomed in his chest. "Fair enough."

Tessa spun in a circle on the worn wood plank stage of the venerable old theater. They'd made it to Nashville the day before and Julia had given a book reading and question and answer session for a crowded auditorium on a local university campus.

Before joining her sister on the road, it had been years since Tessa had seen Julia interact with a live audience. She was impressed at how personally Julia seemed to take every question and situation raised by one of her fans. To Tessa's surprise, Julia hadn't tried to play the big sister card since they'd been together during the past week. Instead, she treated Tessa as an equal and made sure that everyone involved in the tour gave Tessa a huge amount of respect for her contributions to Julia's success.

Maybe it was the change in her sister or maybe the change was in Tessa. She no longer felt like the weaker sister. Her time in Starlight had done that. And in truth she had to give a lot of the credit to Carson. His belief in her and the fact that he never treated her as less than capable had helped kick-start the change in her.

She no longer felt like she had to dress a certain

way or wear a specific kind of makeup in order to be seen as the person she wanted to be. She understood that came from the inside and believed in herself, full stop. She wished she could thank him. She wished she could call him and tell him about the funny things that happened on tour. The towns she'd visited and what she liked about each of them.

In the bottom of her suitcase, she had several little trinkets she'd bought because the souvenirs reminded her of Lauren. She might never have the opportunity to give them to the girl. But she couldn't help thinking of her. She missed them both more than was healthy.

"I remember how much you liked to sing when you were really little," her sister said. "Maybe you should join a local band in Starlight or wherever you end up."

"Maybe I will." Okay, that was a stretch. But at the moment Tessa felt like anything was possible. "You know June Carter and Dolly Parton and Trisha Yearwood and a host of other country music wonder women have performed on this stage," she told her sister. "Being in a place like this makes me feel strong."

"You are strong, Tessa."

She whirled at the sound of Carson's deep voice, then threw an accusatory glance at Julia, who was standing upstage.

"I'm going to give you two a minute," her sister said with a wink.

Tessa was so shocked she couldn't even respond. She just stared at Carson. "What are you doing here?" she asked finally.

"I wanted to talk to you in person," he said. "Your sister helped me coordinate it."

"I'm going to kill her."

"She told me you'd say that." He chuckled although it sounded forced.

"This isn't funny." Not when her heart was hammering in her chest and it felt like all the walls she'd erected since he'd hurt her were tumbling down like nothing more than a child's blockhouse.

He immediately sobered. "I know it isn't funny. I know I hurt you, Tessa. I'm so sorry. You have no idea how sorry I am."

"Forgiven," she blurted. "Now I need to go."

"Please don't. Please just hear me out. You've been so strong. Braver than me at every turn. Please don't walk away now."

She drew in a steadying breath and swallowed back the emotion rising in her throat. "Where is Lauren?"

"She's staying with Ella until I get back," he said.

"My friends are in on this, too? I'm not sure who to kill first."

"I made a horrible mistake. I hurt you because I

was scared. Because you made me feel too much. Because I wanted things with you that I didn't think I deserved."

She could hear the sincerity in his tone, and she wanted to believe him. She wanted to forgive him. To forget about everything that had gone before and start over.

She shook her head. "I don't think I can do it again," she said honestly. "Not when my heart could be broken one more time. I understand that you have to protect Lauren, but I need to start standing up for myself. I need somebody who wants me for the person I am. Not because I fit in a certain mold or because I don't make waves or mistakes. I'm going to make mistakes, Carson. I have learned that above everything else. But I'm a good person. I'm a person worthy of love. I'm worthy of somebody risking everything to love."

He took a step closer to her. "I know that, Tessa, and I want to be that person. Give me a chance to be a man who deserves you."

"What happens when things get rough?" she asked. She took a breath then added, "There are no guarantees, Carson. I could get sick again. The scare I had with my doctor turned out okay, but there are no guarantees in life."

"I know that. And I don't care. I welcome the good stuff and the bad." He ran a hand through his cropped hair. "You know, Tessa, I'm not exactly coming to you without baggage. I have a kid. And an ex who is potentially not going to make things easy. I never should have doubted you when it came to Lauren. I'm so sorry for that. It turns out, my daughter is a lot smarter than her old man. She understood how good you were for us from the start."

"I love that kid," Tessa whispered because what else could she say?

"And what about her father? Is there any chance you could find it in your heart to try again with me? I'm not saying it'll be perfect. I'm not expecting you to let me in fully. I know I need to earn my way back. But I want a chance to try. If there's any possibility, please give me that chance."

She lifted a hand to her mouth when a small sob escaped.

"I still love you," she said. "I wish it were easier to stop loving you."

He walked toward her slowly like he was giving her a chance to tell him to stop. Like he was once again putting the choice in her hands. She didn't tell him to stop. She took a step forward, meeting him in the center of this stage.

"You are strong and brave and beautiful. I swear that I will do better."

"You help me feel strong," she told him honestly.

"I was able to be brave because I saw myself through your eyes."

"What do you see in my eyes now?"

He crouched down so they were eye to eye. What she saw there took her breath away.

"Love," she whispered.

"Along with a healthy mix of fear," he said. "I've never been good at letting people in. You and Lauren are teaching me how to be vulnerable and how to love. But I can't do it without you, Tessa. I need you so badly."

She lifted a hand to his rough cheek. His skin was warm, and awareness rippled through her body. She'd missed every part of him.

"You have me." She gave a watery laugh. "I think you've had me since that day in the hot springs."

"I've had a lot of fantasies about the hot springs," he said with a smile. "I have plans for you and those hot springs. Will you come home with me, Tessa? Please come home."

"Yes." The word was a promise and an oath. Before she could say more, he claimed her mouth as he took her into his arms. The kiss was a rediscovering and a reawakening. It felt like coming home.

Tessa knew this man would always be her home. No matter what they faced in life, or what challenges or successes came their way. They would be a home for each other. Forever.

Epilogue

Two weeks later, Tessa stood on the sidelines of the soccer field in Starlight, holding her breath as she watched a girl from the opposing team dribble the ball down the field. Lauren's team was up by a score of three to two with less than a minute left in the game. Her heart hammered in her chest as she glanced from the determined midfielder to the goal where Lauren stood at the ready.

At least Tessa hoped the girl was ready. What she really hoped was that one of the defenders on the team would stop the other girl before she got a shot.

She could hear Carson on the other side calling

out words of encouragement. A big change from where he'd started as a coach.

So many changes for both of them, and she welcomed every one, feeling confident that their love would see them through whatever life threw in their way.

They'd returned to Starlight together after his declaration of love. Although she would continue to work for her sister and meet Julia at certain tour stops throughout the summer, there was no doubt that Tessa's future belonged with Carson and Lauren in Starlight.

She'd even invited her parents to come and visit over the Labor Day holiday, ready to introduce them to the person she'd become since moving away from home.

She knew she would have found a way to make a happy life for herself even if she and Carson hadn't reunited, but the fact that she could move forward with him made everything that much sweeter.

Although the only thing she cared about now was the pint-size midfielder dodging the girls on Lauren's team like some kind of soccer prodigy.

It was the final game of the season, and Tessa knew how much it meant to Lauren to end on a win. She also understood the valuable lessons that could be learned from overcoming adversity.

After meeting with the pediatrician and the allergist, Lauren had agreed to switch to goalie, and they'd started on a new treatment for her asthma, one that seemed to be working well based on the fact that the girl hadn't had another flare-up.

Tessa cheered and forced herself to take in a gulp of air as the final defender made a lunge for the ball. She kicked and missed as the midfielder executed an impressive pivot. Then there was nothing between her and the goal but Lauren.

Time seemed to move in slow motion as the girl drew back her foot and kicked, sending the ball soaring toward the right goalpost.

At the last moment, Lauren jumped and caught the ball in her hands, rolling clear of the goal as she held it to her chest.

The whistle blew to signal the end of the game, and the team and fans went wild. The girls surrounded Lauren as she stood and held the ball above her head with the triumphant whoop of excitement.

Carson and the other mom who helped coach ran on to the field as well and he swept his daughter into his arms for a congratulatory hug.

Tessa waited on the sidelines with the rest of the spectators. She couldn't remember ever feeling so much happiness and relief mixed together.

After the team huddle, Lauren and Carson walked toward her, both of them grinning wildly. She gave

Lauren a huge hug. "That was the best thing I've ever seen," she told the girl. "You were amazing."

"Thank you for helping me practice," the girl said, hugging her back. "I knew just where she was going to kick the ball because it's where you always kick the ball."

Tessa chuckled. "I'm afraid I don't do it on purpose, but I'm glad it helped." She winked at Carson. "Congratulations, Coach. I think this calls for a celebratory ice cream."

"It sure does," he agreed. "But we have something to talk to you about first."

"Don't tell me this is more negotiating for a puppy." Lauren had been trying to convince the two of them to make a trip to the local animal shelter since they'd returned.

"It's a different kind of commitment," Carson said. "And I'm not sure this is the best place for it, but it was mentioned that I still owe you a grand gesture and…" He held out his hands. "This is as grand as it gets in my life."

Tessa glanced over her shoulder to see Madison and Ella standing a few feet behind her. She felt her eyes widen as she tried to figure out why they would be here at this moment. Cory and Jordan had left for their honeymoon, but neither of her other friends had mentioned stopping by today.

She quickly returned her gaze to Carson, who

looked strangely nervous as he dropped the soccer equipment bag onto the grass. "Is there a problem with..." She didn't want to finish the sentence and upset Lauren at this moment. Delilah was still being difficult about a custody agreement, although her boyfriend's band had decided to record the new album in Ibiza instead of Nashville. Definitely not a place for Lauren to even think of joining them.

"No problem," he promised then cleared his throat. "But no matter what challenges we might face, Tessa, I want to do it at your side."

"You complete us," Lauren shouted as she grabbed first her dad's hand and then Tessa's. "Sarabelle says that's the line we have to use."

Tessa rolled her lips together as she tried to keep a straight face. "It worked for Tom Cruise," she agreed.

"I love you, Tessa Reynolds." Carson took a small step closer to his daughter. "We both love you and we want to spend the rest of our lives together."

In tandem, father and daughter dropped to one knee as Carson pulled a small velvet box out of the side pocket of the equipment bag.

"You put it in with the soccer balls?" Madison called out. "Smooth move, Campbell." Her teasing elicited a round of laughs from the players and their families that were now watching with avid interest.

Tessa kept her eyes trained on that box. Her heart was once again beating at a ferocious pace and it felt as though her whole body were filled with the flutter of butterfly wings.

"I don't have the smoothest moves," Carson acknowledged, "but I love you with my whole heart and everything I am."

"Me, too," Lauren echoed.

He flipped open the box to reveal a beautiful round diamond flanked by two smaller stones in an antique setting. The ring was perfect, just like the moment.

"I love you both so much." Tessa lowered herself to her knees as well.

"Let him ask the question," Ella said. "Make the man work for it."

"Every day of our lives," Carson promised. "I'll work to love and cherish you *every day*. If you'll have me."

"Us," Lauren clarified.

"Will you marry us?" Carson asked.

"Daddy." Lauren shook her head as she grinned at Tessa. "You'll marry him but be my step mommy."

"Yes," Tessa whispered. "A million times yes."

He slipped the ring onto her finger and then pulled both her and Lauren into a tight hug as their friends cheered.

Everything about the moment was perfect, and Tessa knew without a doubt that her life had led her to this place. All of the challenges and surgeries and setbacks had made her into the person she was, the woman who Carson loved. She would treasure each day and the life she planned to build with the single dad and daughter who had captured her heart.

* * * * *

For more stories of seizing the life you want with both hands, try these other great romances from Harlequin Special Edition:

She Dreamed of a Cowboy
By Joanna Sims

Dreaming of a Christmas Cowboy
By Brenda Harlen

Available now from Harlequin Special Edition!

WE HOPE YOU ENJOYED THIS BOOK FROM

HARLEQUIN
SPECIAL EDITION

Believe in love. Overcome obstacles. Find happiness.

Relate to finding comfort and strength in the support of loved ones and enjoy the journey no matter what life throws your way.

6 NEW BOOKS AVAILABLE EVERY MONTH!

#2893 ANYONE BUT A FORTUNE

The Fortunes of Texas: The Wedding Gift • by Judy Duarte

Self-made woman Sofia De Leon has heard enough about the old-money Fortune family to know that Beau Fortune is not to be trusted. And now that they are competing for the same business award, he is also her direct rival. It is just a hot Texas minute, though, before ambition begins warring with attraction...

#2894 FIRST COMES BABY...

Wild Rose Sisters • by Christine Rimmer

When Josie LeClaire went into labor alone on her farm, she had no one to turn to but her nearby fellow farmer, Miles Halstead. Fortunately, the widowed Miles was more than up to the task. But a marriage of convenience is only convenient until one side ends up with unrequited feelings. Will Miles be willing to let go of his fears, or will Josie be the one left out in the cold?

#2895 HOME IS WHERE THE HOUND IS

Furever Yours • by Melissa Senate

Animal rescue worker Bethany Robeson already has her hands full with an inherited house and an overweight pooch named Meatball. She doesn't dare make room for Shane Dupree, her former high school sweetheart, now a single dad. Bethany doesn't believe in starting over, but Shane, baby Wyatt and Meatball could be the family she always dreamed of...

#2896 THE WRANGLER RIDES AGAIN

Men of the West • by Stella Bagwell

For years, rugged cowboy Jim Carroway has been more at home with horses than with people. But when stunning nanny Tallulah O'Brien arrives to wrangle the kids of Three Rivers Ranch, she soon tempts him from the barn back to life. After Jim lost his pregnant wife, he thought he'd closed his heart forever. Can the vibrant, vivacious Tally convince him that it's never too late for love's second act?

#2897 THE HERO NEXT DOOR

Small-Town Sweethearts • by Carrie Nichols

Olive Downing has big dreams for her Victorian bed-and-breakfast. She doesn't need her handsome new neighbor pointing out the flaws in her plan. But Cal Pope isn't the average busybody. The gruff firefighter can be sweet, charming—and the perfect partner for the town fundraiser. Maybe there's a soft heart underneath his rough exterior that needs rescuing, too?

#2898 A MARRIAGE OF BENEFITS

Home to Oak Hollow • by Makenna Lee

Veterinarian Jessica Talbot wants to build a clinic and wildlife rescue. She could access her trust fund, but there's a caveat—Jessica needs a husband. When she learns Officer Jake Carter needs funding to buy and train his own K-9 partner, Jessica proposes. Jake is shocked, but he agrees—only for the money. It's the perfect plan—if only Jessica can avoid falling for her husband...and vice versa!

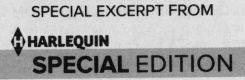
"I remember. I remember it all, Bethany."

Jeez. He hadn't meant for his voice to turn so serious,
so reverent. But there was very little chance of hiding his
real feelings when she was around.

"Me, too," she said.

For a few moments they ate in silence.

"Thanks for helping me here," she said. "You've done
a lot of that since I've been back."

"Anytime. And I mean that."

"Ditto," she said.

He reached over and squeezed her hand but didn't let
go. And suddenly he was looking—with that seriousness,
with that reverence—into those green eyes that had also

kept him up those nights when he couldn't stop thinking about her. They both leaned in at the same time, the kiss soft, tender, then with all the pent-up passion they'd clearly both been feeling these last days.

She pulled slightly away. "Uh-oh."

He let out a rough exhale, trying to pull himself together. "Right? You're leaving in a couple weeks. Maybe three tops. And I'm solely focused on being the best father I can be. So that's two really good reasons why we shouldn't kiss again." Except he leaned in again.

And so did she. This time there was nothing soft or tender about the kiss. Instead, it was pure passion. His hand wound in her silky brown hair, her hands on his face.

A puppy started barking, then another, then yet another. The three cockapoos.

"They're saving us from getting into trouble," Bethany said, glancing at the time on her phone. "Time for their potty break. They'll be interrupting us all night, so that should keep us in line."

He smiled. "We can get into a lot of trouble in between, though."

Don't miss
Home is Where the Hound Is *by Melissa Senate,*
available March 2022 wherever
Harlequin Special Edition books and ebooks are sold.

Harlequin.com

HSEEXP0122B

Get 4 FREE REWARDS!

We'll send you 2 FREE Books plus 2 FREE Mystery Gifts.

Harlequin Special Edition books relate to finding comfort and strength in the support of loved ones and enjoying the journey no matter what life throws your way.

FREE
Value Over
$20

Don't miss the next book in the Wild River series by *USA TODAY* bestselling author

JENNIFER SNOW

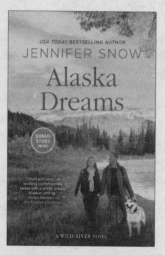

Is she making the right decision...for her heart and her career?

"An exciting contemporary series debut with a wildly unique Alaskan setting." —*Kirkus Reviews* on *An Alaskan Christmas*

Order your copy today!

SPECIAL EXCERPT FROM

HQN

*Rom-com queen Selena Hudson is following her dream
to produce and star in an edgy psychological thriller.
When her leading man drops out at the last minute,
Gus Orosco steps into the role, and their chemistry—
on- and off-screen—is hot enough to melt the Alaskan
snow. If only he weren't strictly off-limits...*

Read on for a sneak peek at
Alaska Dreams,
the newest book in Jennifer Snow's Wild River series.

"What exactly are you doing, anyway?" Gus asked. He
could hazard a guess...

"It's a casting call," Kaia said, sounding like it was the
most exciting day in her young life. She was practically
vibrating on the seat, while obviously attempting to
appear cool and unaffected. It wasn't working.

"For which role?" He hadn't seen many people at the
campsite...mostly just the crew. Were they seriously
hoping to cast a full movie with local talent? That was
ambitious.

Selena hesitated. "The leading male character."

He frowned. "You left LA, where everyone and their
dog wants to be an actor, just to try to find someone to
star in your movie in Wild River?"

She huffed, holding her pen like a dagger. "What's
your point?"

He shrugged. It was none of his business, and that pen could do some damage. "No point. Good luck with it," he said as he turned to head toward the pool tables, where Levi stood waiting. He widened his eyes and sent the guy a look. Levi laughed.

"I still can't believe Levi is friends with that guy," he heard Selena mumble, and he stopped.

Just keep going. Who cares what she thinks of you?

He turned back. "I'm sorry, what?"

She shook her head and smiled pleasantly. "I said, have fun playing pool."

"Thought that's what you said." He continued toward the back of the bar and glanced over his shoulder. Unfortunately, she glanced over hers at the same time. The electricity vibrating between them was undeniable, and he wasn't sure why they continued to bicker. He could just steer clear of her and she could ignore him, but the verbal sparring had him feeling more alive than he had in weeks. Her stare burned with such an intensity that it was almost impossible to look away.

Was she checking him out right now? Or plotting his death? Hard to tell. And damn if that didn't excite him.

Firecrackers was what his grandfather had called the women whom the men in the family were attracted to, and Selena Hudson definitely fell into that category.

Don't miss
Alaska Dreams,
available February 2022 wherever
HQN books and ebooks are sold!

HQNBooks.com